英美诗歌导读

Selected Readings in British and American Poetry

主 编 唐根金 万 华
副主编 丁卫国 马兴暖

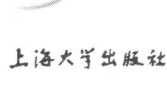

上海大学出版社

图书在版编目(CIP)数据

英美诗歌导读 / 唐根金,万华主编. —上海:上海大学出版社,2014.8
ISBN 978-7-5671-1393-0

Ⅰ.①英… Ⅱ.①唐… ②万… Ⅲ.①诗歌欣赏－英国－高等学校－教材－英、汉②诗歌欣赏－美国－高等学校－教材－英、汉 Ⅳ.①I561.072②I712.072

中国版本图书馆 CIP 数据核字(2014)第 171145 号

责任编辑 陈 强
封面设计 施羲雯
技术编辑 章 斐

英美诗歌导读

主 编 唐根金 万 华
副主编 丁卫国 马兴暖

上海大学出版社出版发行
(上海市上大路 99 号 邮政编码 200444)
(http://www.shangdapress.com 发行热线 021-66135112)
出版人:郭纯生

*

南京展望文化发展有限公司排版
上海上大印刷有限公司印刷 各地新华书店经销
开本 890×1240 1/32 印张 6 字数 139 000
2014 年 8 月第 1 版 2014 年 8 月第 1 次印刷
ISBN 978-7-5671-1393-0/I·245 定价:22.00 元

目录

序言 / 1

第一章　诗歌与人生 / 1
第二章　诗歌与爱情 / 20
第三章　诗歌与战争 / 40
第四章　诗歌与死亡 / 58
第五章　诗歌与城市 / 78
第六章　诗歌与田园 / 99
第七章　诗歌与政治 / 120
第八章　另类的诗歌 / 146

附录　诗人谈诗 / 162

序　言

　　何谓诗歌？或者，究竟诗歌为何？关于这个问题，似乎颇有点老生常谈的意味。说起诗歌，一般读者的反应不外乎如下几点：第一，诗歌属于高度凝练的语言艺术，它所推重和追求的是 Less is more 的境界。第二，诗歌的灵魂是意象，大凡上乘的诗作无不透出作者或雄奇奔放，或轻灵曼妙的丰富想象。第三，诗歌讲究音效，其韵律节奏，包括词语的选择和搭配都关乎独到的音韵美。或许，我们还可以再加上第四点，即诗歌是情感抒发的载体。借用华兹华斯的话来说，"诗歌是强烈感情的自然流露，它源于宁静中累积起来的情感"。(Poetry is the spontaneous overflow of powerful feelings; it takes its origin from emotion recollected in tranquility.)的确，就传统的标准来衡量，无论中西，诗歌的基本构成要素大概如此。比如，中国现代诗人何其芳就曾指出，"诗是一种最集中地反映社会生活的文学样式，它饱和着丰富的想象和感情，常常以直接抒情的方式来表现，并且在精炼与和谐的程度上，特别是节奏的鲜明上，它的语言有别于散文的语言"。英国浪漫主义诗人拜伦也曾留下过这样的名句，"诗歌是想象的岩浆，喷发出来足以阻止一场地震"。(Poetry is the lava of the imagination whose eruption prevents an earthquake.)

　　不过，以上关于诗歌的印象只涉及了诗歌的一个方面，尚不足以概括诗歌的全貌。或者,我们可以说,它们仅仅代表了诗歌的外壳和表象。千百年来,诗歌之所以长盛不衰,之所以当得上文学皇冠上的明珠的美誉,除了它精致的语言、巧妙的结构和充满张力的想象以外,根本的原因还在于它是一种灵魂的吟唱,这才是诗歌的本质和精髓。一首好的诗歌,固然往往能够给读者带来感官上的愉悦和满足,但与此同时,它更应该以自己独特的方式融入读者的心灵,唤起或崇高或真诚或喜悦甚或忧伤的种种至情至性。诗歌,有各种各样的目的,它可以是一种呈现或再现,也可以是一种阐释或解读,但它的最高境界无疑应该是一种激动或感动。以罗伯特·海顿(Robert Hayden)的《那些冬天的星期日》(*Those Winter Sundays*)为例,这首诗看似十分不起眼,既没有夸张的意象,没有强烈的音乐感,也没有华彩的语言,给人的感觉甚至不太像诗歌。但是,细读之下,我们会发现,这绝对是一首发人深省的好诗,不仅有深度和力度,更具有心灵的震撼度。全篇从儿子的角度出发娓娓道来,倾吐了对父亲的歉疚之情,饱含着对父亲一份迟到的爱。收尾的两句"What did I know, what did I know /of love's austere and lonely offices?"尤其令人唏嘘感叹:爱有时竟是那么的沉重、那么的孤独无助!只不过,亲人之间的爱、陌生人之间的互敬互爱和相互理解恰恰是现代社会关系中所最稀缺的。诗人在这里虽然写的是亲情,但他呼唤的其实是人情,是人间的大爱。这就是这首普普通通的小诗的魅力所在,也是它能够备受读者推崇的缘由所在。

诗歌的作用还不止激动和感动,它还能涵养心灵、陶冶情操,培育健全和积极向上的人格力量,引导人们对社会和人生开展有益的思考。伊丽莎白·毕晓普(Elizabeth Bishop)曾写过一首《一种艺术》(*One Art*)。在这首诗里,诗人把关注点对准了人生道路上的一次次"失去",她反复告诫自己(同时也在告诫读者),如何面对"失去"是一种艺术,而这种"失去的艺术并非难以掌握"。这是何等的胸襟和气魄,又需要何等样的人生历练才能达到的境界啊!可以想象,如此机巧智慧的文字必定早已在读者的内心引起共振。再比如,英国诗人鲁德亚德·吉卜林(Rudyard Kipling)的那首著名的《假如》(*If*),也真正当得上字字珠玑,处处闪耀着理性的光华。我们在此不妨选取其中的两小节,以一窥其哲理性的高度:

> If you can dream—and not make dreams your master;
> If you can think—and not make thoughts your aim,
> If you can meet with Triumph and Disaster
> And treat those two impostors just the same:
> If you can bear to hear the truth you've spoken
> Twisted by knaves to make a trap for fools,
> Or watch the things you gave your life to, broken,
> And stoop and build'em up with worn-out tools;
>
> ……
>
> If you can talk with crowds and keep your virtue,
> Or walk with Kings—nor lose the common touch,
> If neither foes nor loving friends can hurt you,
> If all men count with you, but none too much:
> If you can fill the unforgiving minute
> With sixty seconds' worth of distance run,
> Yours is the Earth and everything that's in it,
> And—which is more—you'll be a Man, my son!

不过,也有人说,诗歌在当下已经落伍、已经 out。它要么过于抽象、过于偏执,要么过于矫情、流于平庸,它那略显僵化、刻板和慢条斯理的特质与社会发展的趋势和人们的期许正渐行渐远。那些质疑诗歌的人们看起来自有他们的理由,而且,还是冠冕堂皇的理由。人类已经迈进了 21 世纪的第二个十年,在全球化浪潮的大背景之下,在商品经济不断发酵的氛围里,特别是在互联网一波又一波的冲击面前,无论在古老的东方,还是在西方欧美国家,社会的总体形制,包括上层建筑和意识形态,人们的日常生活以及他们对精神产品的追求无不发生了巨大的变化。一方面,人们生活的节奏变得更快、更紧凑,学习、工作、养家糊口的压力比以往任何时候都要大。为了更加美好的生活,每个人都忙忙碌碌,已没有多少余暇时间可以慢慢地品味文学。另一方面,随着互联网和其他新媒体的普及,比如,电子杂志、在线阅读平台、网上论坛、微博、QQ、微信等,一种所谓的快餐文化应运而生,成为时尚的滋养心灵的通途。相形之下,文学落寞了,诗歌也沦落到了被淘汰的边缘。近些年来,文学杂志的不景气、乃至停刊,诗集出版数量的下降以及诗歌读者群的萎缩等就可资佐证。

那么,诗歌是否真的就此消沉了呢?是否果真失去了它的用武之地呢?或者说,究竟应该如何,才能为诗歌争得一席生存和发展的空间呢,才能让诗歌的血脉得以传承下去呢?这一连串的问题,当然并非三言两语就能轻松地解答。不过,有一点是确定无疑的,我们相信,诗歌不会消失。诗歌或许会产生分化,事实上,诗歌的改良和变革从未间断过。诗歌或许会趋于更加多元,写诗的人们也不会仅仅满足于文字的游戏,诗歌的概念也一定会被植入新的元素,但诗歌不会沉沦。时代固然在飞速前进,诗歌的位置仍不容取代。即便诗歌似乎已无奈从文学的圣坛跌落,难再回到往昔的辉煌和荣光，但只要真与美还在，只要那一份感动和激动还在，诗歌就有希望。还是让我们来读一读狄金森的这首小诗吧：

> There is another sky,
> Ever serene and fair,
> And there is another sunshine,
> Though it be darkness there;
> Never mind faded forests, Austin,
> Never mind silent fields-
> Here is a little forest,
> Whose leaf is ever green;
> Here is a brighter garden,
> Where not a frost has been;
> In its unfading flowers
> I hear the bright bee hum:
> Prithee, my brother,
> Into my garden come!

多么恬淡、宁静、高远的画面啊！诗歌里或许什么也没有，但却有纯美的"另一片天空"，这就足够了！这也是我们编写这本《英美诗歌导读》的原初动力所在，因为我们仍向往那诗意盎然的"另一片天空"。不仅如此，我们还愿意通过这本小书引导大家认识诗歌、走近诗歌，真切地感受诗歌的魅力。

最后，就本书的编写作一个简单的说明。《英美诗歌导读》一书由唐根金、万华、丁卫国、马兴暖、王瑶、罗梦琦、董晓亚、丁文杰和卢亚等同志共同参与编写，其中主编唐根金、万华，副主编丁卫国、马兴暖。成书过程中,得到了上海大学外国语学院周平院长、冯奇副院长和庄恩平副院长的热情关心、鼓励和帮助,特表示衷心的感谢。上海大学出版社陈强编辑也为本书的出版提供了有力的支持和帮助,在此一并表示感谢。

唐根金

2014 年 2 月 11 日

写于内布拉斯加林肯大学的 Andrews Hall

第一章

诗歌与人生

点 题

Poetry is life distilled.

—— Gwendolyn Brooks

诗歌与人生，一个历久弥新的话题。多少年来，无论中西，醉心于文字的诗人们无不以手中生花的妙笔，或重彩浓墨、或如蜻蜓点水一般轻轻勾勒，兼容并包、博采众长，书写了一幅幅活色生香、独具特色的人生百态图。英国女诗人玛丽·奥利弗（Mary Oliver）曾经指出，"诗歌并非职业，它是一种生活方式。它就像一只空空的篮子，你把自己的人生投入其中，即会有所收获。"（Poetry isn't a profession, it's a way of life. It's an empty basket; you put your life into it and make something out of that.）这句话精妙之极，可谓道尽了诗歌与人生（或者说生活）之间关系的种种。

首先，诗歌来源于生活，这一点是毋庸置疑的。拥有什么样的人生、何等样的生活态度和生活经验，就会写出什么样的诗歌。比如，有"新英格兰农民诗人"美誉的弗罗斯特，他的作品之所以呈现出简约、清新、富于生活气息的特点，就与其丰富的人生阅历（弗罗斯特当过工人、送报员、乡村教师，经营过农场等），特别是多年的新英格兰乡村生活经历密不可分。弗罗斯特虽然出生在美国西部的大城市旧金山,但他人生中几个主要的阶段却是在偏远的新罕布什尔州农场度过的。因此,他的不少脍炙人口的名作,包括《割草》(Mowing)、《修墙》(Mending Wall)和《雪夜林边小驻》(Stopping by Woods on a Snowy Evening)等不但渗透着浓郁的田园意趣和乡土情结,还真实地反映了生活在这片土地上的人们的日常生活和所思所想。当然,诗歌的目的绝非简单地描摹生活、刻录人生。但凡优秀的诗歌,必然是源于生活又高于生活。也就是说,诗人的使命不应仅仅是再现和复制;更重要的是,他需要凝练和萃取,并在此基础上,与读者分享他的心灵感应和人生体验。拿弗罗斯特来说,他固然是一位长于表现自然和质朴的乡村生活的诗人,但在另一方面,他的诗歌的哲理性、意蕴绵长和引人深思才是成就他诗坛地位的根本所在。

第二,经由生活浸润的诗歌反过来又回馈和报偿生活。诗歌是文学艺术的集大成者,在诗歌里,人们可以把玩文字的旷世奇美,可以聆听高山流水之音,可以搭乘想象的翅膀悠游四方,也可以悄无声息地陶醉在或深刻或恬淡或热情似火或温婉动人的意境之中。培根所谓"读诗使人灵秀"(Poets make men witty)或许指的就是诗歌的这一特殊功能。凭借辞藻、修辞、意象、节奏和意义等等,诗歌能够为读者营造一片纯净的天地,能够给人们带来心灵的愉悦和至高无上的享受,能够怡情养性、促成健全人格的培养。换言之,它对提升生活的品位、丰富人生的内涵均大有裨益。以爱伦·坡的《安娜贝尔·李》(Annabel Lee)为例,诗中唯美的意境衬托出的淡淡的哀愁以及婉转悠扬的调子不知打动了多少读者的心。再比如,济慈的《希腊古瓮颂》(Ode on a Grecian Urn),且不说这首诗中包含了几多瑰丽的想象、浓烈的色彩感和凹凸有致的立体感以及丰富的审美意蕴和深刻的思想,单就其中的一个警句"美即是真,真即是美"(Beauty is truth, truth beauty)就足以证明它摄人心魄的力量。再举一个例子,狄金森曾写过一首小诗,叫做 There is no Frigate like a Book。这是一首非典型的狄金森作品,它的内容无关爱情、无关上帝,也无关生死永恒之类的命题。虽然只有短短的八行,但是,通过三个巧妙的比喻,诗人把读者惬意地领进了书本的天地和知识的殿堂,这就是诗歌反馈给生活的最好的礼物。

第三,诗歌的作用除了呈现、分享和给人以美学意义上的享受之外,还有另一种更高层次的表现,那就是引导人们思考,激发人们对生活的热情,从而为个人生活和社会生活提供精神上的推动力。诗歌是开放性的,从形式到内容,可以说无所不包。以人生为主题的诗歌,可以写幸福、快乐和青春飞扬,也可以写痛苦、迷惘,甚至死亡。但是,即便是探讨苦涩和不堪重负的人生体验,其终极目的仍然必定是传递希望和给人以向上的力量。所谓不朽的诗篇,都有一个共同点,那就是通篇闪耀着人性的光华。以弥尔顿的《论失明》(On His Blindness)为例,这是英国文学史上最为著名的十四行诗之一,也是诗人在双目失明、家庭遭遇不幸、人生处在大劫难的背景下写成的。诗歌取名《论失明》,一开始也的确道出了因"失明"而起的惆怅和失落。不过,诗人随后笔锋陡转,不但表达了身处逆境时宝贵的豁达平和,更吟唱出了信心、决心和勇气。也正是凭着这一种巨大的精神力量,才使他在看不见光明的情形之下完成了《失乐园》、《复乐园》和《力士参孙》等传世名篇。多恩(John Donne)的《神圣十四行诗之十》(Holy Sonnet X: Death, Be Not Proud)也是一个被广泛引用的例子。这首诗作的高妙之处在于对待死亡的超然态度,总体的调子既是激愤的,也是洒脱不

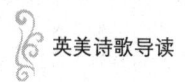

拘和痛快淋漓的。其所揭示的生与死的辩证关系,实质无非是告诫人们要学会踏踏实实地生活,等到死亡来临之时,才能够坦荡荡地勇敢面对。

最后,从某种意义上来说,所有诗歌(甚至所有的文学作品)都堪称关于人生的一曲颂歌。人世间的风风雨雨、人生道路上的无数历练和体验,尽可以在诗歌这本大书中找到对应的页码。诗歌里有爱情有亲情有友情,有野心勃勃有温情脉脉,有慷慨大义有阴谋也有权术,有喜悦有悔恨也有懊恼不已,有对过去的追忆也有对未来的憧憬,有乡土风情也有异国情致,有如花的少女也有粗鄙的莽夫,有战争有毁灭有死亡有痛苦,等等。这就是诗歌,用英国作家海兹利(William Hazlitt)的话来说,"诗歌是生活中一切值得谨记的东西"(Poetry is all that is worth remembering in life.)。

本章是本书的开篇第一章,收录了不同时期的四位英美(丹尼斯·莱弗托夫是英裔美籍诗人)诗人各自的代表性诗作。这些作品有的侧重具体的人生体验,有的是在咀嚼人生之后发出的感悟和感叹,还有的则涉及对人与人之间、人与社会之间关系的冷峻思考等。我们希望,这些作品将不仅帮助读者领略到英美诗歌的魅力,同时也为自己的人生打开一扇智慧的窗。

名篇导读

1. My Papa's Waltz[①]

Theodore Roethke

The whiskey on your breath
Could make a small boy dizzy;

But I hung on like death:
Such waltzing② was not easy.

We romped until the pans
Slid from the kitchen shelf;
My mother's countenance③
Could not unfrown itself.

The hand that held my wrist
Was battered on one knuckle;
At every step you missed
My right ear scraped a buckle.

You beat time④ on my head
With a palm caked hard by dirt,
Then waltzed me off to bed
Still clinging to your shirt.

【诗人简介】西奥多·罗特克(Theodore Roethke, 1908—1963),美国二十世纪四五十年代最著名的诗人之一,出生在一个德国移民家庭。主要诗集有:《开门的房屋》(1941)、《丢失的儿子及其他》(1948)、《觉醒》(1953)、《替风辩护》(1958)等。

【注释】
① 此诗选自作者1948年出版的带有自传性质、体现诗人成长经历的诗集《丢失的儿子及其他》(*The Lost Son and Other Poems*)。

② waltz：一般作名词，意为"华尔兹舞"，标题中即为名词。此处的 waltzing 为动名词，作主语用，意为"跳华尔兹舞"。第四节第三行中的 waltzed 则为动词的过去式。

③ countenance：面容；脸色；表情。

④ beat time：打拍子。

【作品赏析】

《爸爸的华尔兹》是美国诗人西奥多·罗特克的名作之一，一般认为该诗具有明显的自传色彩。

作品从儿子的角度出发，回忆了小时候和父亲一起随着华尔兹的节奏手舞足蹈的情形。父亲是个出卖劳力的普通工人，他的双手粗糙难看，其中一个手指关节甚至开裂了。像大多数重体力劳动者一样，他在收工回家之后，也喜欢端起酒杯咪上几口。不过，很显然，在这个家庭里还有一项特殊的活动，或者说是自娱自乐的活动，它不但帮助父亲解除一天劳作的疲乏，也足以令当时尚少不更事的儿子铭记一生。这项活动就是在一家人吃过晚饭之后，由父子二人和着华尔兹的曲调，开心而又滑稽地翩翩起舞。父亲的嘴里喷着酒气，他或许已有了几分醉意，而儿子的身高也仅够到父亲的腰间。显然，这样的华尔兹，实际不过是转圈罢了。但是，父子二人却乐此不疲，特别是儿子，即便歪来扭去不时要擦碰到父亲的皮带扣子，也心甘情愿。他们快活地转来转去，不小心碰翻了厨房的餐具，结果惹得母亲也发了急。但是，母亲并非真的有心责怪。锅碗瓢盆奏出的交响乐，加上一高一低扭在一起的父子同乐场景，还有什么比这更温馨、感人和其乐融融的家庭生活氛围呢？

父亲的影响对孩子一生的成长至关重要。这首诗歌，看似平淡无奇，实则感情充沛，饱含着儿子对父亲的爱和思念，洋溢着温暖人心的巨大力量。

整首诗共分为四节,每节四行,以 abab 形式押韵,读来朗朗上口。值得一提的是,作品在选词和词语搭配方面特色鲜明。为了与作品所透出的浓郁生活气息相呼应,诗人在用词上不但力求鲜活、生动,贴近生活的本真,而且还不忘营造诙谐幽默的效果。比如,第一节第三行的 hung on like death 和全篇最后的 Still clinging to your shirt 就活灵活现地刻画出了一个孩子对父亲的依赖、崇拜和对与父亲一起跳狂野华尔兹的渴望。此外,第二节最后一行中双重否定的使用也给人以眼前一亮的感觉。父子之间的疯癫华尔兹看着固然有喜感,但是,只有随着这个家庭里女主人的粉墨登场(虽然只是间接的出现),这一幅普通人生活的图景才会变得完整和丰满。

2. The Ache of Marriage[①]
Denise Levertov

The ache of marriage:

Thigh and tongue, beloved,
Are heavy with it[②],
It throbs in the teeth

We look for communion
And are turned away, beloved,
Each and each

It is Leviathan③ and we
In its belly
Looking for joy, some joy
Not to be known outside it

Two by two in the ark④ of
the ache of it.

【诗人简介】丹尼斯·莱弗托夫(Denise Levertov, 1923—1997),英裔美籍女诗人,一生著有20多部诗集,作品主题丰富,多涉及社会问题(如越战和女性主义浪潮等),风格上也变幻多姿,受美国先锋派诗人影响较多。

【注释】

① 此诗选自英裔美籍女诗人丹尼斯·莱弗托夫于1964年出版的诗歌集《哦,品赏发现:新诗集》(*O Taste and See: New Poems*)。

② 此处的it以及随后出现的几个it均指the ache of marriage。

③ Leviathan:《圣经》中象征邪恶的海怪,常以鲸鱼、鳄鱼等形象出现。有时音译为"利维坦"。

④ ark:此处即指圣经《创世纪》里面提及的"诺亚方舟"(Noah's Ark)。

【作品赏析】

古罗马的西塞罗曾经说过,"婚姻是社会的第一份契约。"(Marriage is the first bond of the society.)就个人而言,婚姻常被认为是位列生和死之后的人生第三大事件。婚姻的本质究竟是什么,婚姻与爱情是否相互排斥,怎样才能谋求长久而又幸福的婚姻,诸如此类的问题历来为文人和哲学家们所津津乐道。英裔美国女诗人丹尼斯·莱弗托夫写下的这首《婚姻之痛》可以说是这方面的又一个尝试。

这首诗歌以一个"痛"(ache)字起始,似乎为婚姻生活的本质早早定下了基调。从第二行到第四行,女诗人把处于婚姻中的男女所经受的种种痛楚比作牙疼,可谓用心良苦。牙疼虽乃寻常之事,但是,经年累月的疼痛个中滋味实非外人所能体察。在随后的三行中,倒不见 ache 或指代 ache 的 it 出现,不过,细读这三行(We look for communion/And are turned away, beloved/Each and each),实质在意思上与 ache 无异,甚至更进一步。这里固然写到了夫妻双方试图交流和沟通,惜乎结局依然苦涩。这对男女徒有夫妻的名号,却始终无法真正走到一起,他们的内心不具有兼容性,而是存在着距离感。及至最后的两个小节,作者接连运用了两个源自《圣经》的典故,不但继续强化"婚姻之痛"的主题,同时也增加了作品的厚度,丰富了作品的层次感。Leviathan 多以怪诞和可怖的面目示人,它的出场喻示婚姻恰似一个温柔的陷阱,或者是一个迷雾重重的圈套,令人感到难以捉摸、无所适从,最后无奈在婚姻的围城里左冲右突,却始终不得其门而出。不过,随后出现的 ark 却笔锋陡转,传达出了别一番深意。ark,亦即拯救人类于危难的 Noah's Ark,它是希望和救赎的象征。可见,在女诗人看来,即便婚姻里有困惑和苦痛如影随形,但希望犹在,信心犹存,惟有于苦中寻乐,痛并快乐地执着前行,才有可能觅得幸福的妙谛。

整首诗歌以女性特有的质感和细腻的笔触,真实地还原了无数男女所不容回避的婚姻生活中的窘境。全篇节奏和缓,语调克制平和,但又不乏灵活和弹性,读来引人深思。

从创作技巧的层面来看,这首诗歌的特点之一是诗行的长短不一以及小节与小节之间行数的不规则。这样的处理,或许可以理解为与婚姻所呈现的起伏和波折相呼应。另外,诗中一些意象的构建也别具韵味。比如,Thigh and tongue 的组合,貌似牵强滑稽,但在此处却有点睛之妙,可谓一言道尽了婚姻中的貌合神离和同床异梦。最后,得益于 ark(诺亚方舟)的意象以及 Two by two (成双成对)所带来的效应,使得诗歌的结尾呈现开放性的特征,为读者的思考留下了无限的空间。

3. I'm nobody! Who are you?[①]

Emily Dickinson

I'm nobody[②]! Who are you?
Are you nobody, too?
Then there's a pair of us
Don't tell — they'd banish us, you know.

How dreary to be somebody!
How public—like a frog—
To tell your name the livelong[③] June
To an admiring bog[④]!

【诗人简介】艾米莉·狄金森(Emily Dickinson,1830—1886),19世纪美国最重要的诗人之一,惊人的创作力使她为世人留下了1800多首诗,但在她的有生之年,作品未能获得青睐。直到美国现代诗兴起,她的成就才获得认可,并被赞誉为现代新诗运动的先驱。

【注释】

① 此诗首次刊印于1891年出版的美国女诗人艾米莉·狄金森的《诗歌集:第二辑》(Poems, Series 2),该诗集由 Mabel Loomis Todd 和 Thomas Wentworth Higginson 协助编辑出版。

② nobody:即中文所谓的"无名之辈",它与第二节首行中的 somebody 恰好相反,后者意为"大人物"或"重要人物"。

③ livelong:意为"整个的"、"全部的"。

④ bog:沼泽,泥塘。

【作品赏析】

此诗在艾米莉·狄金森全部近2 000首诗歌中并不算最出名的,若要论读者的认知度和阅读喜好,*Because I could not stop for Death* 和 *I died for Beauty — but was scarce* 应能位居前两位。其他如 *Wild nights! Wild nights*,*Success is counted sweetest*,*My life closed twice before its close*,*"Hope" is the thing with feathers*,*I heard a fly buzz when I died*,*There's a certain slant of light* 和 *Much madness is divinest sense* 等也是受到热捧的狄氏代表性作品。不过,这首 *I'm nobody! Who are you?* 同样是值得一读的绝佳好诗,而且,喜爱它的人们也不在少数,尤其在当下年轻人普遍崇尚个性、拒绝平庸的年代,更是如此。

这首诗歌所最为人称道的是它叛逆的姿态和率性纯真的气派。开篇第一句"I'm nobody! /Who are you?(我是无名之辈!你是何人?)"单刀直入,气势逼人,高调地宣示了"我"的立场。紧接着，在第二和第三行："Are you nobody, too? /Then there's a pair of us.（你也是无名之辈吗？/那我们算是一伙的了。）"这表明"我"不但自己乐意当一个默默无闻的小人物，也渴望找到意趣相投的同路人。第四行是"我"对同伴的善意的告诫："Don't tell—they'd banish us, you know（别声张，你知道的，他们会赶我们走。）"总的来看，第一小节的这四行围绕"无名之辈"展开，落笔张扬又不失轻巧，字里行间还透着风趣、俏皮和调侃的意味。第二小节关注的重点转向"大人物"，但是，"我"一开始即断言"当名人多无聊"，这与此前愿作"无名之辈"时的洒脱和怡然自得形成了强烈的反差。随后的三行更进一步点明，为何贵为"重要人物"竟至于这般了无生趣。在这里，作者巧妙地设计了两个互相关联的类比：一是把所谓的名人比作喋喋不休、扰人清静的青蛙（frog），二是把只懂得盲目崇拜名人，却迷失了自我的芸芸众生比作泥沼（bog）。青蛙的鸣叫不具有任何实质意义，它只会惹人厌烦；从另一个角度来说，也只有那一摊烂泥才最适合当它的听众。可见，在"我"的内心里，所谓出人头地、追名逐利终究是徒劳无益的虚妄之举，唯有朴实平淡、活出真我的本色才是生活的本源。全篇虽仅短短八行，但主题雄奇奔放、不落俗套，风格清新自然，反映了女诗人超乎常人的异质禀赋。

从写作手法的层面来看，这首诗歌也体现出典型的狄氏风格。首先，与狄金森的绝大多数诗作一样，这首诗歌原本也没有标题。此处我们把它的首行用作标题，这是通行的做法。第二，这首诗歌的诗行比较简短，多为三个音步或四个音步（而英诗中最常见的长度为五音步的诗行，即 pentameter），这也是狄金森习惯采用的长度。第三，就押韵而言，此诗未见严格的韵脚形式（第六和第八行除外），相反，行间韵（internal rhyme）和半押韵（slant rhyme）则比较多见。比如，第五行里的 dreary 和 somebody 就是一个行间韵的例子。再比如,第二行和第四行最后的 too 和 know 可以被看作是半押韵的例子。需要指出的是,在狄金森所处的时代,严格的韵律是一般诗人在创作中力求遵循的原则。但是,狄金森却是一个例外。这也是狄氏区别于其他同时代诗人的所在,体现了她的独特性和创新精神。第四,此诗延续了女诗人一贯的手法,以第一人称的"I"出发展开叙述,同时,结合 we、us、you 和 your 等人称代词的使用,给读者营造出一种现场感和急迫感。第五,标点符号的创新使用也是狄金森诗作的一大特色。比如,在这首诗歌中,就可以看到各有三处出现了破折号和感叹号。

4. Fable[①]

Ralph Waldo Emerson

The mountain and the squirrel
Had a quarrel;
And the former called the latter "Little Prig[②]".
Bun[③] replied,
"You are doubtless very big;
But all sorts of things and weather
Must be taken in together
To make up a year
And a sphere[④].
And I think it no disgrace
To occupy my place.
If I'm not so large as you,

You are not so small as I,
And not half so spry.
I'll not deny you make
A very pretty squirrel track;
Talents differ: all is well and wisely put⑤;
If I cannot carry forests on my back,
Neither can you crack a nut."

【诗人简介】拉尔夫·瓦尔多·爱默生(Ralph Waldo Emerson, 1803—1882),美国哲学家、散文家、诗人,新英格兰超验主义的杰出代表。他的作品深刻隽永,说理深入浅出、简单明晰,体现出典型的"爱默生风格"。主要作品有《论自然》、《诗集》、《五月节及其他诗》等。

【注释】

① 此诗曾被收录进由 Thomas R. Lounsbury 编辑,于 1912 年出版的《耶鲁美国诗歌集》(*Yale Book of American Verse*)。

② Prig:自以为是或自命不凡的家伙,含贬义。

③ Bun:此处即指松鼠。

④ sphere:原意为"球体"、"天体",此处有"天地万物"的意思。

⑤ all is well and wisely put:该句大意为"世间万物,各有其所长"。

【作品赏析】

一般认为,爱默生以散文名世,其代表作《论自然》、《论美国学者》、《散文一集》、《散文二集》和《论超灵》等影响深远。但不可否认,爱默生同时也是一位重要的诗人。只不过长期以来,他的诗歌才能为其超验主义思想和散文方面的巨大成就所掩盖,未能引起读者和评论界应有的重视。

爱默生一生写下过不少风格清新脱俗、富于哲理性的诗篇,其中的大部分收录在1847年和1867年出版的两本诗歌集里。他曾被朗费罗(Henry Wadsworth Longfellow)称为"思想的歌者"(singer of ideas),可见,在他的诗歌体系中,睿智、启迪和思想的火花代表了他创作的符号。他的诗歌总体而言看似不事雕饰、平淡无奇,但字里行间往往透出逼人的智慧光华。这一点与他的散文创作可谓有异曲同工之妙。

《寓言》(*Fable*)一诗是典型的爱默生式的作品。全篇采用拟人化的手法,围绕高山和松鼠之间的"论战"(quarrel)展开。高山和松鼠,一大一小,南辕北辙,可以说几乎是风马牛不相及的两个事物。按一般常理,它们之间本不具备任何可比性,更遑论要打起"嘴仗"。但是,爱默生自有他的独出心裁之处。他巧妙地把这一组看似强弱对比明显、不在同一层级上面的对象并置在一起,在双方矛盾的交错中层层推进,并最终通过松鼠——这一貌似处于不利地位的弱者之口——道出了作者的所思所想。原来世间万物,各有其值得称道之处。正所谓"尺有所短,寸有所长"。大,固然有大的好处,但却不应该"恃大而傲",目空一切。小,也绝对不乏小的功用和妙处,完全不必因此而妄自菲薄,悲悲戚戚。这就是生活的定律,也是人生所应该追求的真谛。

从具体的写作手法来看,这首诗歌也体现出了相当的反传统特点。首先,它没有分小节(全诗共19行),诗行长短不一,短句偏多。其次,它虽有韵脚,但并未呈现严格意义上的押韵模式。第三,它的语言相对通俗易懂、贴近日常生活,没有所谓"诗歌的语言"(poetic language)的痕迹。凡此种种,与作者所处时代一般通行的诗歌创作路数多有不同,与其作为散文大家的风格倒有几分神似。此外,作品取名"寓言",堪称点睛之笔。

总之,这是一首节奏简洁畅快、调子轻松幽默的哲理小诗。作品从细微处入手,不疾不徐,不惊不乍,虽蕴含着简单而又深刻的人生大道理,却全然不见空洞乏味的说教。诗中的一些警句,如 Talents differ:all is well and wisely put 以及 If I cannot carry forests on my back, Neither can you crack a nut 等,已成为人们传诵的名句。

小 结

诗歌即人生,人生也常常被比喻成是一首诗。诗歌可以是鸿篇巨制、气势磅礴、一泻千里,也可以是小桥流水、曲折委婉。而人生固然有轰轰烈烈、大起大落,有时却也不乏平平淡淡、从从容容。诗人莱昂纳德·科恩曾经说过:"诗歌是生活的证明。若你的人生充分燃烧,那么,诗歌就是燃烧过后留下的灰烬。"(Poetry is just the evidence of life. If your life is burning well, poetry is just the ash.)

浏览英美文学史,经过熊熊燃烧之后留下的"灰烬"一路洒满了大西洋两岸的广袤地带。从英国方面来说,其有记载的最早的文学作品是英雄史诗《贝奥武甫》(*Beowulf*)。这部在现在看来艰涩难懂的煌煌大作,虽然夹杂着不少宗教的元素,却是反映早期英伦三岛人们智慧、勇敢、顽强生活的原始读本。到了 14 世纪,随着乔叟(Geoffrey Chaucer)的出现,英国历史上第一位伟大的诗人诞生了。乔叟的《坎特伯雷故事集》(*The Canterbury Tales*)以浪漫、传奇和亦庄亦谐的调子相衬托,凭借活泼灵动的描写,形象地再现了中世纪晚期英国社会生活的风貌。书中的人物,从高贵的骑士到贫贱的农夫,从尊荣的女修道院长到口无遮拦的巴斯妇人,各行各业各色人等,无一不活灵活现、呼之欲出。乔叟之后,荣耀登场(且至今从未谢幕)的自然首推莎士比亚。莎士比亚的十四行诗(共154首)是英语文学的瑰宝,字里行间闪耀着光华夺目的人生大智慧。从青春到爱情、从瞬间到永恒、从人生的美好到死亡的悲悯和痛苦,凡此种种,在莎翁的笔下,可以说应有尽有。即便是他的那些用韵文写成的悲剧、喜剧和历史剧,抛开文字的精美和人物的丰满厚实不说,当中也富含对人生的不同感悟和多重解读。比如,在《麦克白》(Macbeth)第五幕中,当主人公麦克白得知妻子死讯后,就曾发出过"人生只是痴人说梦的玩意,充斥着吵闹和喧嚣,实质却毫无意义"(It is a tale told by an idiot, full of sound and fury, signifying nothing.)的著名悲叹。浪漫主义诗歌是英国文学的又一个高峰,期间名家名作迭出,布莱克、华兹华斯、济慈、拜伦、雪莱等,光是粗略地列出一串名单就已足够震撼。当然,他们的作品也都离不开人生这个宏大的主题。此后,伴随着维多利亚时期文学的繁荣,以及19世纪末20世纪初西方文明的转型和发展,英国更成为现代诗歌运动的策源地。诗歌与人生的大戏,始终在一幕幕精彩地上演着。

就美国而言,固然它的文学传统和积淀不能与英国相提并论,却也诞生了无数的传奇。北美大地上第一位具有里程碑意义的诗人无疑是安妮·布雷兹特里特。这位处事低调的女诗人曾创作了不少歌颂生活、爱情的优秀作品,至今令人难忘。还有一位朗费罗,他的作品可算得上是中国读者心目中必读的诗歌。他的《人生礼赞》(A Psalm of Life)曾经激励、并仍在激励无数年轻人。爱伦·坡是另一位重量级的人物。虽然他自己的个人生活似乎并不有序、也不得意，但是，他以旷世的才情在诗歌里为我们构筑了一个美轮美奂的世界，在这里真善美是永远的主旋律。谈到美国诗歌，特别是19世纪的美国诗歌，狄金森和惠特曼是两座绕不过去的高峰。前者睿智、内敛，后者豪迈、奔放、乐观、大气磅礴，绝对都是顶级的生活艺术家。进入20世纪，美国诗歌呈爆发式发展态势。因其超级大国的地位，因其对民主和自由的自我标榜，因其商品经济和多元文化的特质，诗歌得以脱颖而出，成为反映美国社会政治经济文化甚至娱乐潮流的一个风向标。从强调传承欧陆文化到渴望建立美国本土特色，从推崇"非个人化"到坚持书写个人经验，从对语言的精雕细琢到融汇不同的艺术门类，美国诗歌走过了一条不平凡的道路。与此同时，它与美国国内此起彼伏的政治和文化运动也有着千丝万缕的联系，从民权运动到女性主义，从反文化到同性恋，从反战到生态保护，都可以见到诗歌的影子。还有各种新潮的理论、文艺（包括电影、音乐、绘画和摄影等）潮流等，也对诗歌的走向产生了巨大影响。以收入本章的两位美国诗人为例，罗特克虽然不见得是站立潮头、一呼百应的扛旗式人物（他被公认为20世纪最有影响力的诗人之一，2012年，曾和其他9位诗人一起出现在美国邮政印刷的邮票上），也不太容易被归入哪一个体系或派别，但显然他十分看重书写个人经验，《爸爸的华尔兹》就是典型的例子。怪不得评论家认定，罗特克的诗歌以善于反思和咀嚼人生而得名。莱弗托夫的诗歌成就以她在1947年嫁给美国作家古德曼以后的作品为主，作品中有"黑山派"的影子，也可以看到反对越战、主张女性主义诉求等的影响。她的这首《婚姻之痛》，因其女性诗人的身份，完全可以被当作女性主义的宣言书来解读。

当然，回望英美诗坛，区区几首小诗远不足以反映其全貌。正因为如此，在"扩展阅读篇目"的环节，我们列出了部分与本章主题相关的名家名篇,希望起到一个延展和补充的作用,为读者开展下一步的阅读提供一些线索。

扩展阅读篇目

Those Winter Sundays by Robert Hayden

A Psalm of Life by Henry Wadsworth Longfellow

Leisure by William Henry Davies

One Art by Elizabeth Bishop

Invictus by William Ernest Henly

"Hope" Is the Thing with Feathers by Emily Dickinson

On His Seventy-Fifth Birthday by Walter Savage Landor

Gather ye Rosebuds while ye may by Robert Herrick

My Heart Leaps up When I Behold by William Wordsworth

On His Blindness by John Milton

Ode on a Grecian Urn by John Keats

Annabel Lee by Edgar Allan Poe

Holy Sonnet X: Death, *Be Not Proud* by John Donne

She Walks in Beauty by Lord George Gordon Byron

When I was one-and-twenty by A.E. Housman

第二章

诗歌与爱情

点 题

Poets always end up talking about love, the frail magic mystery of a lover's silent tenderness.

—— e.e. cummings

　　爱情是文学永恒的主题，而关于爱情，最简洁、最直观、最多姿多彩的表达方式无疑是诗歌。诗歌不仅凭借其弹性的结构和多维的视角使表现爱情有了各种各样的可能，同时，还以其精致凝练的语言为读者体察爱情之美留下了巨大的空间。纵观人类历史长河，我们从来没有停止过对爱情追求和探索的脚步，诗人们更是以他们特有的浪漫情怀和才思谱写了一曲曲美不胜收的爱情篇章。中国可以说是一个诗的国度。在中国诗歌的发展历程中，以爱情为主题的诗歌数不胜数。从最古老的典籍《诗经》中的感情炽热到汉魏六朝爱情民歌的细腻婉转，从唐代最具代表的李商隐的《无题》组诗到宋代肝肠寸断的相思词句，无不体现了诗歌创作中爱情这个主题举足轻重的地位。

　　在西方文学史上，爱情诗亦是一道亮丽的风景线，它以瑰丽多姿的风貌和经久不衰的审美价值吸引了历代的读者。就英美的诗

第二章
诗歌与爱情

歌传统来看,爱情是一个既古老又新鲜的话题,诗人们以各自对爱情独特的理解和体悟,始终在孜孜不倦地开展全方位、多角度的探索,抒写着他们心目中爱的真谛。回望过去,历代的英美诗人中,描写爱情的高手比比皆是。他们笔下的爱情或温馨甜蜜,或伤感忧愁;感情的宣泄或热烈奔放,或含蓄内敛。每位诗人的诗歌都以其独特的艺术魅力在文坛绽放出夺目的光彩。

爱情是人类最高尚和美好的情感,说起爱情,人们首先会联想到爱的甜蜜欢乐、温馨和谐。英美诗歌中自然也少不了这方面的佳作名篇。诗人们通过细腻的笔法或赞叹爱人的花容月貌,或描绘与爱人共处时的柔情蜜意,或憧憬和回忆爱的浪漫与狂热,这众多情感都汇成了感人肺腑的情诗绝唱。莎士比亚在其第 130 首十四行诗 *My mistress' eyes are nothing like the sun* 中就把自己的爱人同世上所有美丽的事物相比较,虽承认爱人的眼睛不如太阳明亮、嘴唇不如珊瑚红艳、胸脯不如雪般白净、脸颊不如玫瑰粉嫩等,但他就是爱不完美的她,诗人毫不掩饰地赞美着他的爱人,倾吐出对所爱之人的一片痴情。罗伯特·彭斯的 *A Red, Red Rose* 是一首经典的爱情诗,字里行间洋溢着一种饱满圆润的爱的气息,全篇的基调蓬勃热烈,表达了诗人对恋人花容月貌的景仰和对永恒爱情的热切期盼。

诗歌创作的一个最大特点是抒情,却人各有法、诗各有异。爱情是美丽的,但也并非总是浓情蜜意,爱情的忧伤和喜悦总是交织在一起,才让人无法忘怀。在爱情的王国里,热恋时的温馨与甜蜜虽是诗人经常赞美的,但是恋人的离别却也永远都是最令人伤感的话题。中国古诗中素有"多情自古伤离别"的无奈,无独有偶,这种伤感以及由此而引出的别样的美同样也反映在西方诗歌当中。美国女诗人艾米莉·狄金森的 *I cannot live with You* 和 *So We* must meet apart 寄托的恐怕就是这样一份无可奈何。所谓爱情,有时免不了要面临山穷水尽的窘境,等到耗尽了所有的热情,剩下的就只有苦涩的遥遥相对。那些无望的爱似乎总有排山倒海一般的巨大力量,既累人,更伤人。在狄金森的这首诗中,女诗人写出了一种忧郁的心绪,一种无奈的痛苦。爱情的失意使人饱尝人世酸楚,她祈祷能得到解脱,但收获的却往往是无尽的伤感、绝望以及独自承受离别之痛的重压。

除了以上列出的这些描写热恋时的甜美快乐和离别时的伤感惆怅的诗歌,在英美诗歌体系中,也有相当一部分作品赞美了爱情的坚定与永恒。在莎士比亚的第 116 首十四行诗中,诗人就认为,爱是亘古长明的灯塔,是指引方向的恒星。真正的爱情应该能经得起时间的考验,顶得住生活中暴风雨的袭击,能做到同甘共苦、坚韧执着,只有在挫折和磨难中相互扶持的爱情才是真正的爱情。诗人站在人性的高度,歌颂了纯真的爱情。同样在约翰·多恩的经典爱情诗 A Valediction: Forbidding Mourning 中,诗人也阐述了相似的观点。他强调精神之爱,认为真正的爱情不在于两人的长相厮守,只要两个灵魂融为一体,执着地坚持着,就不会在乎暂时的分离。哪怕一方走到天涯海角,两人依然会像圆规的两个支点那样,相互牵连,相互依存。

本章从众多描写爱情的优秀诗人中选取了最具代表性的五位:克里斯蒂娜·罗塞蒂、叶芝、勃朗宁夫人、安妮·布雷兹特里特和威廉·布莱克,对其诗作进行详尽的解读和分析。爱情是诗人灵感的源泉,在所选的五首诗歌中,诗人们分别从不同的角度表达了各自对爱情的不同感受和态度。接下来,就让我们一起走进这五位诗人的内心世界,去感受他们用最动人的语言所呈现出的绝美爱情吧。

名篇导读

1. Remember[①]

Christina Rossetti

Remember me when I am gone away,
Gone far away into the silent land;
When you can no more hold me by the hand,
Nor I half turn to go yet turning stay.
Remember me when no more day by day
You tell me of our future that you plann'd[②]:
Only remember me; you understand
It will be late to counsel then or pray.
Yet if you should forget me for a while
And afterwards remember, do not grieve:
For if the darkness and corruption leave
A vestige[③] of the thoughts that once I had,
Better by far you should forget and smile
Than that you should remember and be sad.

【诗人简介】克里斯蒂娜·罗塞蒂（Christina Rossetti，1830—1894），英国诗人。她的抒情诗平易纤巧，哀婉动人，富于音乐节奏感。主要作品集有《妖魔集市》(1862)、《王子的历程》(1866)等。

【注释】

① 此诗选自作者1862年出版的诗集《妖魔集市及其他诗集》

（Goblin Market and Other Poems）。

② plann'd：相当于 planned。

③ vestige：意即"残余"。此处的 a vestige of the thoughts 意为"过去的想法"。

【作品赏析】

克里斯蒂娜·罗塞蒂是英国 19 世纪最伟大的女诗人之一，当年曾被誉为"伦敦第一才女"。弗吉尼亚·沃尔夫（Virginia Woolf）说过："在英国女诗人中克里斯蒂娜·罗塞蒂名列第一位，她的歌唱得好像知更鸟，有时又像夜莺。"的确，如果说她的宗教诗不免给人以沉稳有余而轻灵不足的印象的话，那么，她的爱情诗则又是另一番景致：婉转悠扬、清丽脱俗，有时又如泣如诉，哀婉动人，无论把它们比作知更鸟的歌声还是夜莺的啼唱都是再恰当不过的了。

此诗写于诗人与所挚爱的男友告别之际。开篇第一行就已经铺垫出整首诗忧伤的基调。主人公将要离开人世，但她并不恐惧死亡，因为她要去的是 silent land，可以远离人世的喧嚣与繁杂。不过，令她无法释怀的是和自己的爱人阴阳两隔，再也不能感知他手心的温暖。前两节反复出现的关键词 remember me 释放了主人公对爱人以及那段美好岁月的追忆和怀念。诗人忘不了与爱人的牵手，忘不了两人的柔情蜜意，忘不了曾经一起憧憬未来。但相依相伴的岁月将无可奈何地逝去，任何的安慰和祈祷都已无法挽回。因为就要离开了，所以只希望爱人一直记着自己就好。第三节、第四节反复出现的一对反义词：remember 和 forget 提示了诗人为爱全心全意付出的胸怀。因为疼惜爱人，不愿爱人像自己一样饱受思念的煎熬，所以希望对方忘记自己，微笑地继续生活下去，而让这份执着的思念只在自己的心间反复吟唱。整首诗中的关键词 remember 出现了 5 次,反复咏叹,暗示回忆频率之快,次数之多。前 3 个 remember 为首语重复,其所表达的情感层层加深。在最后两句的平行结构中,remember 和 forget 这两种记忆意象的对比组合,smile 和 be sad 这两种情感意象的对比组合,表现出这两对相互对立、矛盾的情感在相互冲撞碰击,从而使全诗充满张力,其中饱含的深深爱意让人不禁潸然泪下。因那份爱"你"的心,"我"可以放弃我最后的念想。在这离别之际,一直埋藏于心底的爱情突然迸发,诗人一改往日的含蓄与矜持,直截了当地表达出了自己的情感。

十四行诗的形式历来是爱情诗的首选。此诗采用的是彼特拉克体(the Petrarchan Sonnet),韵脚为 abba abba cddece。诗中运用了头韵及尾韵,而尾韵中多用双元音和长元音,以着力渲染整首诗所弥漫的令人窒息但又难以摆脱的气氛,使人仿佛感觉到叙述者满腔深沉温柔的爱与内心的痛苦的交织。

作为维多利亚时期杰出的诗人,克里斯蒂娜·罗塞蒂把爱、恨、忧、惧诸多令人悸动难平的强烈情感,提炼成一种纯净平和的情愫,融入轻婉柔美的韵律和节奏之中。她的爱情诗既有哥特式的神秘,又有拜伦式的浪漫。在她貌似平静的吟咏中,奔涌着情感的激流,恰恰是这一点使我们看到一个特别的她,使她达到了众多诗人难以企及的高度。

2. When You Are Old[①]

William Butler Yeats

When you are old and gray[②] and full of sleep,

And nodding by the fire, take down this book,
And slowly read, and dream of the soft look
Your eyes had once, and of their shadows deep;

How many loved your moments of glad grace,
And loved your beauty with love false or true,
But one man loved the pilgrim③ soul in you,
And loved the sorrows of your changing face;

And bending down beside the glowing bars④,
Murmur, a little sadly, how Love fled
And paced upon the mountains overhead
And hid his face amid a crowd of stars.

【诗人简介】威廉·巴特勒·叶芝（William Butler Yeats, 1865—1939），爱尔兰诗人、剧作家和散文家，"爱兰尔文艺复兴运动"的领袖。他的诗受浪漫主义、唯美主义、神秘主义、象征主义和玄学诗的影响，演变出独特的风格，他的艺术代表了英语诗从传统到现代的过渡。

【注释】

① 此诗创作于1893年，是爱尔兰诗人叶芝为其初恋女友、爱尔兰民族解放志士莫德·岗（Maud Gonne）所写的诸多抒情诗中最脍炙人口的一首。

② gray：意为"头发花白的"。

③ pilgrim：此处名词用作形容词，指"朝圣者一般的"、"虔

诚的"。

④ the glowing bars：此处指"燃烧的壁炉"。

【作品赏析】

1889年,24岁的叶芝认识了莫德·岗,并对她一见钟情。叶芝为她写下了大量的情诗,将她比作玫瑰、天鹅、女神,由此展开了热烈的追求。但是,叶芝狂热的爱,却没有得到莫德的丝毫回应。五年之后,依然对莫德念念不忘的叶芝写就此诗。在这首诗中,至情至性的诗人以优雅舒缓的笔触,淡淡地倾吐出一份深入骨髓的爱意,把心中的感伤化成缱绻的诗魂。可以说,这也正是一个29岁的年轻人情到极处的悲喜交响。

全诗以一个假设性的时间状语开头,接着写垂垂老者睡意蒙眬,在炉火旁打盹,后来她取下书架上的诗集细细品读,一边读一边回忆着过去。值得注意的是,所有这些场景与人物的举止都是虚拟的,它们并没有真实地发生在诗人的实际生活中。然而,恰在这些平易朴素的诗句背后让我们感受到了诗人坚持和执着的力量。因为,诗人在写下这首诗之后所经历的情感波折以及此后漫长的岁月,都印证了当初他写这首诗时的感知,诗人仿佛一直义无反顾地朝着自己预设的、虚拟的时空走去,没有热烈宣泄的激动,只有平静而真挚的倾诉。

在这首诗中,第二节的后两句是全诗的诗眼,深刻隽永。时光带走青春、摧毁容颜却也验证真心,许多人爱慕你的青春美貌,只有一个人仍爱着你那颗朝圣者般的心灵和日渐衰老的容颜。超越时光、经受岁月的磨砺而依旧坚如磐石的爱情,才最真切感人。在诗的结尾处,就像电影中的蒙太奇镜头,诗人将回忆的画面推向现实,尤其让人感到一种沧海桑田式的崇高之美。显然,诗人心底那

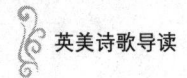

份经过岁月洗礼的真挚情感此刻已变得更加纯净、高远,升华成了永恒的艺术。

  爱情是美好的,歌唱爱情的诗歌可以说俯拾皆是。然而,能突破窠臼、直指人心的则寥寥无几。这首《当你老了》构思精妙,穿越时空,抒发了诗人真挚不渝的感情,表达了叶芝对爱情深刻的领悟,给人以通透的美感。欣赏这首诗,一种感动、一种崇高的美不知不觉进入心灵深处。沧桑过后,容颜已逝,爱情还能如初见时那般真挚坚定吗?叶芝的这首诗为我们诠释了答案:真爱超越时空,超越外在美丑,直至永恒,这正是人们对爱情亘古不变的终极向往与追求。在如今这个物欲横流的年代,风花雪月的浮华表象正掩盖真爱的光芒,许多人在追求真爱的道路上迷失了自己。品读这首诗,使我们有机会重新认识到爱情的真谛,也使我们深深体会到"愿得一心人,白首不相离"的宝贵和不易,它唤醒的不仅是记忆,还有我们对真爱的渴望与追求。

3. If thou must love me, let it be for nought[①]
Elizabeth Barrett Browning

If thou[②] must love me, let it be for nought
Except for love's sake only. Do not say,
"I love her for her smile ... her look ... her way
Of speaking gently, ... for a trick of thought[③]
That falls in well with mine, and certes brought
A sense of pleasant ease on such a day" —
For these things in themselves, Beloved, may

Be changed, or change for thee,—and love, so wrought,
May be unwrought so. Neither love me for
Thine own dear pity's wiping my cheeks dry：
A creature might forget to weep, who bore
Thy comfort long, and lose thy love thereby!
But love me for love's sake, that evermore
Thou may'st love on, through love's eternity.

【诗人简介】勃朗宁夫人(Elizabeth Barrett Browning, 1806—1861),英国诗人,曾被提名为桂冠诗人的候选人。主要作品有《天使及其他诗歌》(1838)、《诗集》(1844)、《葡萄牙人十四行诗集》(1850)、《大会前的诗歌》(1860)等。

【注释】

① 此诗选自勃朗宁夫人于1850年出版的《葡萄牙人十四行诗集》(*Sonnets from the Portuguese*),为其中的第14首作品。此外,该诗集中的第33和第43首诗也十分出名。

② thou：古英语,汝、尔,也即"你"。

certes：古英语,相当于certainly, truly,意即"当然地"。

thee：古英语,thou的宾格,汝、尔,也即"你"。

thine：古英语,thou的所有格,意即"你的"。

thy：古英语,thou的所有格,意即"你的"。

③ a trick of thought：此处可理解为"思想的火花"。

【作品赏析】

《葡萄牙人十四行诗集》是英国著名女诗人勃朗宁夫人的自传

性作品,里面收录的 44 首诗歌都是作者写给丈夫的情诗。这些诗作是诗人曲折情感历程的真实写照,记录了两人之间爱情火苗的点燃、熄灭,进而复燃成熊熊烈焰的全过程。勃朗宁夫人原名伊丽莎白·巴莱特,15 岁时因骑马不幸跌落马背,造成脊椎损伤,只能长期卧床。此后,她博览群书,醉心于诗歌创作,并逐渐崭露头角。39 岁那年,她迎来了年轻诗人罗伯特·勃朗宁的造访。后者对她的才情仰慕不已,还向她发出了明确的爱的讯号,对她展开大胆的追求。伊丽莎白的生命从此揭开了新的篇章。迟来的爱情战胜了阴霾,她那不知疲倦的情人帮她摆脱了惊慌、疑虑和恐惧,扶着她一步步走到了阳光下,而他们两人也终于成就了一段至今让人津津乐道的文坛佳话。

《如果你爱我》是《葡萄牙人十四行诗集》中的第 14 首。作者开篇点题:If thou must love me, let it be for nought/Except for love's sake only,此句统领全诗,奠定了全诗的基调。在勃朗宁夫人看来,爱是无条件的,不是世俗的、功利的。爱就是爱,它应该是简单的、纯粹的。正如诗中所写,爱情不必着眼于 her smile, her look, her way of speaking gently 等等的外在条件。人的外貌会随着时间的推移而衰老,人的心理会随着环境的改变而变化,把不确定的因素当作建立真爱大厦的基础,坍塌只是早晚的事情。诗人还提出了不要因为怜惜而产生爱,温柔的安慰只是代表同情和怜悯,不能把它误认为是爱。在罗列了诸多不能成为爱的理由之后,诗人明确地指出:love me for love's sake。也就是说,爱是不需要理由的,它只是一种纯粹的感性的意念,是一种感觉,是为了爱而爱。最后,诗人表达了愿达到爱情持续永恒的至高境界的强烈愿望:Thou may'st love on, through love's eternity,不禁令人想到中国式的"我欲与君相知,长命无绝衰"的爱的绝唱。全诗在韵律上,除第七句和第十三句外,其主导音步为五音步,基本格调为抑扬格,韵脚为 abba abba cdcdcd,属于典型的彼特拉克式(或称意大利式)十四行诗。作品韵律优美,语言流畅,易于上口。

爱,源于心灵震颤;诗,记录生命体验。对于勃朗宁夫人而言,正是罗伯特纯真的爱才唤醒了那颗深藏心底的诗歌的种子,促成它萌发出强大的生命力,而反过来,诗歌的力量和蓬勃生机又助推了她生命之花的怒放。这首《如果你爱我》,虽只有区区十四行,却是勃朗宁夫人这位文坛奇女子用最虔诚的笔墨谱写的一曲"因爱而爱"的华章,带给我们极强的艺术冲击力与感染力。每每捧读这一篇章,除了体会形式与内容兼得的艺术美,读者的心灵往往也变得更加纯净。虽然勃朗宁夫人的一生颇多坎坷,但是,她的生命无比精彩。她的诗歌因爱而生,因爱而美丽动人,因爱而流芳后世,这就是爱的证明。

4. To My Dear and Loving Husband[①]

Anne Bradstreet

If ever two were one, then surely we.

If ever man were loved by wife, then thee.

If ever wife was happy in a man,

Compare with me, ye[②] women, if you can.

I prize thy love more than whole Mines of gold,

Or all the riches that the East doth hold[③].

My love is such that Rivers cannot quench,

Nor ought[④] but love from thee give recompense.

Thy love is such I can no way repay;
The heavens reward thee manifold, I pray.
Then while we live, in love let's so persever⑤,
That when we live no more, we may live ever.

【诗人简介】安妮·布雷兹特里特(Anne Bradstreet, 1612—1672),北美殖民地的第一位著名诗人,作品成为17世纪新英格兰宝贵诗歌遗产的一部分。她的抒情诗直到19世纪艾米莉·狄金森以前的约两百年里,一直是女诗人作品中的佼佼者。

【注释】

① 此诗选自作者去世6年后、即1678年出版的诗集《几首充满智慧和学识的诗》(*Several Poems Compiled with Great Variety of Wit and Learning*)。

② ye:古英语,尔等,也即"你们"。

③ 在17世纪、18世纪,甚至19世纪,西方人普遍认为,遥远的东方不但是个神秘的所在,而且那里财富遍地。此句意在表明作者对丈夫的爱就算所有的财富也无法比拟。doth:古英语,相当于今天的does。

④ nor ought:相当于not anything。

⑤ persever:即persevere,意为"坚持"。

【作品赏析】

安妮·布雷兹特里特,北美殖民地时期的第一位重要诗人,其于1650年出版的诗集《新近在美洲崛起的第十位缪斯女神》(*The Tenth Muse Lately Sprung up in America*)被认为是移民在北美创

第二章 诗歌与爱情

作的第一部文学作品集。布雷兹特里特的诗歌创作,基本上可以分为两类:一是反映当时盛行的清教主义思想的宗教沉思,二是表现爱情、亲情和友情等与日常生活密切相关的抒情小品。由于当时所处的环境,再加上家庭的氛围,布雷兹特里特是一位虔诚的清教徒,笃信上帝。如果说笃信上帝为她提供了灵魂的归属感的话,那么俗世中的家庭之爱则给她带来了精神的愉悦与物质的满足。这种家庭之爱也是她诗歌中常见的主题,《致我亲爱的丈夫》就是其中有代表性的一首。这首诗歌向读者展示了作者作为一位清教徒对爱情和婚姻的态度。在诗中,她直率而热烈地抒发对丈夫的爱,质朴的措词和略微夸张的语气搭配营造出强烈而真挚的情感效果,使其对丈夫的爱与信赖溢于言表、意切情真。

诗人在开篇连续运用了三个设问句(均以 If ever 开头),不但瞬间点燃了爱的浓情蜜意,同时还散发出浪漫温馨的气息。读罢前四行,人们已不再怀疑,诗人夫妇绝对是天底下最幸福的一对,两情相悦、真心相爱,俨然是潇洒无敌的神仙眷侣。此后的诗句,仍然有力,仍然掷地有声,虽然只是出自一位弱女子之口,但每一句都令人刻骨铭心。与其说她是在对着自己的丈夫表达爱的誓言,不如说她是在向这个世界骄傲地宣布他们俩爱的真切、爱的永恒。管它是"whole Mines of gold",还是"all the riches that the East doth hold",这世间难道还有什么能及得上他们俩爱情的万一吗?但是,走笔至此,仍意犹未尽。在后面的几行,诗人又连着用了几个与买卖相关的词语:recompense、reward、repay 等,其用意自然在强调爱情岂是金钱所能比拟的。最后,全诗的结尾双行"当我们活在世上,让我们爱情长存/当我们不再活着,让我们因此永生"终于为全篇画上了一个圆满的句点:爱是永远,即便生命消失,爱仍然还在。

在韵律的选择上，这首诗采用了英诗中常见的抑扬格五音步（iambic pentameter）的形式，中间略有变化，以避免单调。在写作手法上，作者运用了较多类似平行结构的句式：如第一、二行中的 If ever ... then，还有第七、九行中的 My love is such 和 Thy love is such 以及第十一、十二行中的 Then while we live 和 That when we live 等。此外，夸张手段的运用也是本篇的一大特点，不但有效烘托了气氛，更使作者的爱情表达酣畅淋漓，达到极致。

总之，《致我亲爱的丈夫》堪称是美国文学中一首经典的爱情诗，从中我们可以窥见诗人作为一名妻子和一名清教徒的内心世界。安妮·布雷兹特里特以诗歌的形式表达出了她对生活、婚姻和爱情的感受。当人们为生活奔波劳苦，为上帝刻苦清修时，她用她的诗歌为人们打开眼帘，让人们看到了这世界真实的美与善、温情与希望。

5. Love's Secret
William Blake

Never seek to tell thy love,
Love that never told can be;
For the gentle wind doth move
Silently, invisibly.

I told my love, I told my love,
I told her all my heart,
Trembling, cold, in ghastly[①] fears —

Ah! She did depart!

Soon as she was gone from me,
A traveller came by,
Silently, invisibly:
He took her with a sigh.

【诗人简介】 威廉·布莱克(William Blake，1757—1827)，英国前期浪漫主义诗人，作品包含深刻的哲理性，同时具有神秘主义的色彩。主要诗集有《纯真之歌》、《经验之歌》等。

【注释】
① ghastly：阴森的；可怕的。

【作品赏析】
"从一颗沙粒中见一个世界，在一朵鲜花中见一片天空，在你的掌心里把握无限，在一个钟点里把握无穷。"这是英国早期浪漫主义诗人威廉·布莱克的名句之一。他是英国文学史上最复杂也最有个性的诗人。他才华横溢、敏感聪慧，却在生前备受冷落。也许正因为饱尝了人世间的沧桑，他的诗歌中总带着哲学性的思维，神秘凝重，然而却也不乏孩童般的纯真和朴实。在布莱克一生的创作当中，曾写过不少精美的爱情诗，其中有的表达爱情带来的欢乐和陶醉，有的抒发对爱的深切思念与期待，还有的则描写失恋之后的痛苦凄伤。但是，总体来说，这些诗作长期不为研究者们所重视。

这首《爱的秘诀》是布莱克代表性的爱情诗。全诗共三小节，每小节四行，虽然篇幅短小，但这正反映了布莱克一贯的风格，他擅长以朴素的语言、简单的方式来阐明深刻的道理。在这首诗中，我们没有看到华丽的辞藻，相反，进入视线的多是来自日常生活的普通词汇，如 tell、move、silently、trembling、cold、took、gone 等。此外，这首诗歌中的意象构建也十分有特点：简单、明晰，不露痕迹。"柔风"、"轻叹"、"行经的旅人"，看似就在近旁，但却随时都可能消失不见。就像爱情一样，它固然甜蜜温馨，令人神往，叫人着迷，但却往往难以把握。可以说，这是布莱克式的爱情观，诠释了他对爱情的独到见解。爱情是深埋心中去感受的，是需要悉心呵护的；否则，稍不留意，它便会悄然离去，再也捕捉不到。等到爱情离你远去，剩下的就只能是在孤独与寂寞之中独自品尝苦涩的滋味。整首诗节奏和缓、语调中肯，还揉入了一丝神秘的气息，作为送给已爱、正爱和将要恋爱的人们的"爱的秘诀"再恰当不过。

作为一位伟大的诗人，布莱克为后世留下了丰厚的文学遗产。他的诗歌所特有的美感，特别的表现力，深刻而丰富的思想内涵，对后来的诗人都产生了重大而持久的影响。记得有人说过，在英国，身为剧作家而生在莎士比亚之后，身为诗人又未能在布莱克之前出世，那必定会有"来得太迟"的感叹，由此可见布莱克的影响力。

小 结

古往今来，凡人迹所至，爱无处不在。爱情这朵人类生活中永不枯谢的花朵以其独特的魅力与光彩成为文学作品中恒久吟唱的主题之一，而诗歌作为人类情感表露的方式，也成为表现爱情最好的载体之一。其实，在某种意义上，爱情与诗歌就是一对恋人：诗歌有了爱情的浸润故而青春常在、生机蓬勃；爱情也正因为有了诗

第二章
诗歌与爱情

歌的雕塑才更加美丽、动人。

  本章所选的五首诗歌均可谓英诗爱好者必读的经典之作,但侧重各有不同,有罗塞蒂对爱人把自己永远铭记于心的渴望,有叶芝对心爱之人的矢志不渝,有勃朗宁夫人"因爱而爱"的坚定执着,有布雷兹特里特与丈夫之间的深情款款,更有布莱克对恋人离去的伤感遗憾。在具体的表现手段上,这些诗歌也是各具特色、相得益彰。以意象的运用为例,叶芝的 When You Are Old 中出现了五个相互关联的意象:黑夜、炉火、眼睛、爱神、繁星。夜幕虽已降临,但在冬夜里陪伴主人公的不是孤独与寂寞,而是象征温暖和生命的炉火。在黑暗中能够感知生命的明亮的眼睛,给人浪漫温馨的爱神,更何况还有与人遥遥相伴的繁星。在诗中,每一个意象都在另一个意象的映衬下具有了比自身更丰富的内涵。罗塞蒂的 Remember 也包含了丰富的意象。其中,第二行的"寂静的田园"这一意象耐人寻味。它既可以指远离尘世的冷冷清清凄凄戚戚的所在,也可以象征宗教的禁欲主义的生活方式。这一意象概括了诗人想到自己封闭的爱情将忍受孤独寂寞的痛苦,由此伤感不已。布雷兹特里特的 To My Dear and Loving Husband 也不例外,其中的亮点当然是 whole Mines of gold 和 all the riches that the East doth hold 这两行。通过这两个意象,诗人调动起了读者的视觉和触觉神经,仿佛真的看到了大把的黄金,或者,神秘东方的财富已然触手可及。当然,这一切和她对丈夫那份爱比起来,简直一文不值。

  另外,需要特别一提的是勃朗宁夫人的这首诗歌,除了它的艺术冲击力与感染力,该诗还可以被解读为一个追求高尚平等爱情的女性的心声。诗中所提出的"因爱而爱"体现了强烈的女性独立意识。诗人表明自己追求的是抛开一切世俗礼教束缚的爱情,渴望的是不附加任何条件筹码的平等自由之爱。诗人喊出了自己的心声和对真爱的呼唤。爱本身是永恒的,这样的爱才会亘古常青,不会因时间的消逝而褪色。诗人在这里强调的是不掺任何杂质的纯美之爱,不虚饰,不夸张。只有不分高低贵贱的爱,才能达到爱人之间彼此心心相印,灵魂相融相通的爱的最高境界。

总之,通过上述诗歌,五位诗人向我们展示了他们对于爱的不同的领悟。罗塞蒂让我们感知到爱情要全心全意付出而不求回报,叶芝让我们领悟到真正的爱情不会随着恋人娇美容颜的衰老而消逝,勃朗宁夫人让我们体会到只有"因爱而爱"的爱情才最真挚长久,布雷兹特里特让我们了解到爱情的无价,布莱克更是让我们明白要珍惜有限的时光,不要等到爱情失去之后才追悔莫及,怅然叹息。爱情是美好的,也是无数人所苦苦追求的。不论爱情是给予也好,奉献也罢;是忠诚也好,背叛也罢,它都能让你心甘情愿地去为之付出、为之歌唱。在英美诗歌体系中,论及爱情的诗篇还有很多很多,他们或赞美爱情的伟大,或诅咒爱情的善变,或为爱的山盟海誓而击节,或为爱的肝肠寸断而扼腕,每一首都值得我们去细细品读和感悟。愿普天之下的人们都沐浴在爱的光华里。

扩展阅读篇目

Song to Celia by Ben Jonson

I Am Not Yours by Sarah Teasdale

Love Is Not All by Edna St. Vincent Millay

Song by Christina Rossetti

Sonnet 43—How do I love thee? Let me count the ways. by Elizabeth Barrett Browning

Meeting at Night by Robert Browning

第二章
诗歌与爱情

Parting at Morning by Robert Browning

When We Two Parted by Lord George Gordon Byron

To Helen by Edgar Allan Poe

Sonnet XVIII by William Shakespeare

If You Were Coming in the Fall by Emily Dickinson

Sudden Light by Dante Gabriel Rossetti

Words for Departure by Louise Bogan

Bread and Music by Conrad Aiken

第三章

诗歌与战争

点 题

"滚滚长江东逝水,浪花淘尽英雄……"

历史,是冷冷的金戈铁马踏出的弯弯的路,是浓浓的战火硝烟筑成的厚厚的墙,是滚烫的热血泪水汇成的长长的河。战争,在任何时候、对任何民族都不是个陌生的话题,当然也不会是个轻松的话题。

翻开历史的书,眺望远古的路:从波斯帝国,到全民皆兵的斯巴达城邦,八万罗马人被汉尼拔以半数兵力围歼,他们的后代却在随后的500多年征服了欧洲大陆;从拜占庭王朝、卡洛林王朝,到十字军东征,地中海的权力屡次更迭……而神秘璀璨的玛雅文明甚至没有来得及向世界展示其魅力,就已被欧洲侵略者毁于一旦,只留给后人无穷的悲叹与遐思。

西方如此,有着五千年悠长历史的中国亦复如此。从夏到商再到周,从官渡之战到赤壁之战;从"始"皇嬴政到"始"女皇武则天;从唐宋到元再到明清,从中日甲午海战,到八国联军侵华,从鸦片战争的硝烟到圆明园的大火……战争的阴云似乎从来未曾离去。

那么,战争与诗歌之间又有怎样的纠结呢?在中国,最早的诗歌总集《诗经》里曾有"君子于役,不知其期"、"击鼓其镗,踊跃用

第三章
诗歌与战争

兵"和"王于兴师,修我戈矛"等关于战争的诗句。在西方,影响深远的《荷马史诗》中也不乏对特洛伊战争等宏大场面的详细描述。从英国文学的传统来看,其有记载的最早的文学作品《贝奥武甫》即是一部英雄史诗,里面记载了大量的杀戮和拯救,场面惊心动魄。不妨这样说,战争始终是诗歌(也包括英美诗歌)的一个重大主题,从古至今,莫不如此。

当然,战争诗歌也有一个发展和变化的过程。早期的战争诗歌往往都属于篇幅宏大的史诗和叙事诗一类,其功能大致有三:一是记录战争,或呈现战争;二是为统治者树碑立传、歌功颂德;三是宣扬匡扶正义、得道多助的朴素伦理。而现代的战争诗,无论在形式和内容上,较之以往都有明显的突破。首先,它一般不会是动辄好几百行的鸿篇巨制,所以,就不可能堆积大量具体的战争场面描述,更不可能安排故事情节的铺垫、发展。其次,它的表现形式灵活多样,有以传统的十四行诗体写成的,有虽押韵、但并未严格用韵的诗作,也有完全抛弃传统的作诗法而创作的自由诗。第三,它的主题更多的是反映战争的残酷和对人类的伤害,这是现代战争诗与早期战争诗歌的最大差异。现代的诗人,不像他们的前辈,不再追求场面的铺陈,不讲究故事的曲折离奇,他们对于战争的独特理解与他们所处的时代密不可分。他们把战争写进自己的诗歌,那是因为,他们意识到战争的巨大危害。他们的战争诗,有的从经历战场厮杀的士兵入手,痛斥战争的毁灭性;有的从留守家园的孤儿寡母的角度展开,直指战争对人性的摧残;有的以反讽的手段,警示战争的不可理喻;有的以冷峻的笔触,反思战争对人类文明的扼杀;还有的以嬉笑怒骂的姿态抨击穷兵黩武的政治制度等等。虽视角各有不同,但目标指向是一致的,那就是人类应尽其所能避免战争。正如爱默生(Ralph Waldo Emerson)曾经指出的,

"真正而持久的胜利是和平,而不是战争。"(The real and lasting victories are those of peace, and not of war.)

在英美文学中,有关战争的诗篇不计其数,受到读者推崇的佳作名篇也不在少数。本章挑选了其中最具代表性的四首,希望通过细读、点评和赏析,有助于读者对英美的战争诗歌有一个初步的认识,感知到这些诗作的妙处,体会到诗人们反对战争、渴望和平的心声。

名篇导读

1. The Man He Killed[①]

Thomas Hardy

Had he and I but met
By some old ancient inn,
We should have sat us down to wet[②]
Right many a nipperkin[③]!

But ranged as infantry,
And staring face to face,
I shot at him as he at me,
And killed him in his place.

I shot him dead because —
Because he was my foe,
Just so: my foe of course he was;
That's clear enough; although

He thought he'd 'list④, perhaps,
Off-hand like—just as I—
Was out of work—had sold his traps⑤—
No other reason why.

Yes; quaint and curious war is!
You shoot a fellow down
You'd treat, if met where any bar is,
Or help to half-a-crown.⑥

【诗人简介】 托马斯·哈代(Thomas Hardy, 1840—1928), 英国诗人, 小说家, 早期和中期的创作以小说为主, 晚年以其出色的诗歌开拓了英国20世纪的文学。共有诗集8种, 诗918首, 他的诗冷峻深刻、细腻优美, 具有现代意识。

【注释】
① 此诗作于1902年。
② wet: 此处作动词, 意为"沾湿酒杯", 亦即"开怀畅饮"。
③ nipperkin: 容量为半品脱的小酒杯。
④ 'list: 相当于 enlist, 意为"应征入伍"。
⑤ traps: 意为"家当"。
⑥ half-a-crown: 即 half crown, 旧制英国硬币, 面值相当于30便士。

【作品赏析】
托马斯·哈代是英国文学史上重量级的人物, 他的《德伯家的苔丝》和《无名的裘德》等小说影响深远。与此同时,哈代也是一位多产和优秀的诗人,共出版过8部诗集近千首诗作,其中包括自然诗、战争诗、讽刺诗、感怀诗和爱情诗等。

《他射杀之人》是哈代的名作之一,向来为评论家所看重。此诗从一个士兵的角度出发,描述了其在战场上射杀敌人及之后的心理活动的全过程。杀人,对几乎所有人来说,都绝不是一件简单的事。但在战场上,杀人却是无可回避的。倘若杀死了对手,而又没有丝毫的负罪感,甚至,反倒感觉无上的光荣和骄傲,这也许是职业杀手必备的基本素质。但是,哈代诗中的士兵显然只是个新手,他初上战场,还没有变得杀人如麻,没有学会把杀人看成和吃饭睡觉一样自然而然。这就是为什么他会有犹豫、有自责、有恐惧和不解。可以说,这是一首典型的反战诗,作者借可怜的士兵之口道出了战争的荒诞和可怕。

诗歌开篇即是一个有力的假设:"假如他与我相逢在/一家古老的酒馆中,/我们会坐下来,很快/一起干掉好几盅!"不过,第二小节的一个"But"却把士兵拉回到了现实之中:他们相遇的地点并非酒馆,而是战场,有你没我,有我没你。怎么办?无可奈何之下,士兵开枪打死了敌人。事已至此,本无可厚非,因为一切就是在一种非正常的状态下发生的。可是,士兵却开始苦恼,开始追问。他偏偏要为自己找一个必须杀死对方的理由,一个站得住脚的理由,但最后找到的答案竟是"因为他是我的敌人",仅此而已。为了强调这一点,诗人在第三小节中接连用了两个"because",一方面反映出士兵语流的不连续,以凸显他内心的不确定,另一方面则表达了当事人的自责与无奈。此外,这一小节中先后出现的"Just so"和"That's clear enough",也表明士兵仍试图说服自己,给自己一个安慰的理由。可事已至此,或许他只能如此这般自欺欺人,勉强为自己开脱了。只不过,杀死一个人,对于一个战场的新兵来说,岂是那么容易忘却的一件事情。于是,在第四小节中,他由自己,想到了对方,说不定那个人也和自己一样,没有工作,生计无从着落,只能变卖家当,多可怜!可是,那人却被他杀死了。至此,读者可以明显感觉到,士兵对杀人一事仍无法释怀。最后一节,凭借一个"yes",这名士兵以极其肯定的语气得出了结论:"quaint and curious war is!"战争是如此的奇怪与荒谬,它能让你去杀死一个原本可以成为好朋友的人。原本,"我们"可以在酒吧里畅饮,或者我会借给他一些钱。可是,现在一切都来不及了。诗歌结尾处,再次提到了"如果",和开头的假设形成呼应,极具心理震撼力。

就创作手法而言,这首诗体现出不少哈代诗歌的特点,那就是既传统、又现代。具体来说,它的结构比较规则,每节四行,韵律齐整,此其一。第二是它的说理方式,简洁流畅,不露痕迹,融大道理于小故事之中。第三是词汇和句式的选择,作者刻意选用了一些生活化的用语和普通的句式,以和诗中主人公卑微的身份相匹配。最后,在一些修辞手段(如重复)的使用上,功力非凡。

总之,这是一首值得推荐的战争诗中的经典,它以细腻、深刻、冷峻和言简意赅的笔触剖析了战争的残酷性和不可理喻。战争不但剥夺人的生命,还摧毁了人的精神品质和道德力量。

2. War is Kind[①]

Stephen Crane

Do not weep, maiden, for war is kind.
Because your lover threw wild hands toward the sky

And the affrighted steed② ran on alone,
Do not weep.
War is kind.

  Hoarse, booming drums of the regiment③,
  Little souls who thirst for fight,
  These men were born to drill and die.
  The unexplained glory flies above them.
  Great is the battle god, great, and his kingdom —
  A field where a thousand corpses lie.

Do not weep, babe, for war is kind.
Because your father tumbled in the yellow trenches,
Raged at his breast, gulped and died,
Do not weep.
War is kind.

  Swift, blazing flag of the regiment,
  Eagle with crest of red and gold,
  These men were born to drill and die.
  Point for them the virtue of slaughter,
  Make plain to them the excellence of killing
  And a field where a thousand corpses lie.

Mother whose heart hung humble as a button
On the bright splendid shroud④ of your son,

Do not weep.

War is kind.

【诗人简介】斯蒂芬·克莱恩(Stephen Crane,1871—1900),美国文学家,美国现代主义诗歌的先驱。他的诗写法自由,不顾传统的音节与韵律,风格质朴简洁,常通过寓言式的意象揭示生活的真理。有诗集《黑骑者》(1895)和《战争是仁慈的》(1899)。

【注释】

① 此诗选自斯蒂芬·克莱恩于1899年出版的同名诗集,为其中的第69首作品。

② steed:诗歌用语,相当于horse,意为"奔马"、"骏马"。

③ regiment:(军队的)团级单位。

④ shroud:裹尸布。

【作品赏析】

战争,与之相伴的字眼往往是"残酷"、"血腥"、"杀戮"、"死亡"等,而这首诗却被冠以《战争是仁慈的》这样的标题。读者难免会产生疑问,"为什么,难道战争真的是仁慈的吗"?别急,读完之后,你会恍然大悟:战争绝非仁慈。战争的残酷不仅给亲历其中的士兵带来苦难,也给他们的亲人带来了无限的悲伤。原来,在这一标题中,诗人为了表达出强烈的反战情绪,采用了反讽的手法。

在第一节和第二节中,诗人劝姑娘不要哭泣,因为战争是仁慈的。年轻人生来就该战死沙场,那是多大的荣耀! 战争是仁慈的,战神是伟大的,它使年轻人找到了施展拳脚的舞台,有了实现抱负的一片天地! 可是,且慢,细细品读,你会发现诗人实质是愤怒的,战争的仁慈是虚假的。姑娘的心上人不幸遇难,受惊的战马独自狂奔,姑娘的心在落泪、滴血。如果没有战争,亲爱的,你就不会离我而去,我们可以朝朝暮暮、天荒地老。然而,这一切现在都不可能了,是战争摧毁了一切,你的生命,我们的幸福!和人的生命与幸福比起来,战争的荣耀算得了什么呢?在这里,诗人为我们刻画了姑娘为心上人哭泣的画面,"悲痛"已不足以表达诗人的情感,"悲怆"会不会更好一点呢?战争即使是仁慈的,也是不可理喻的,可人都没了,又何谈荣誉呢?

第三节和第四节中,诗人把镜头对准了孩子。请注意,诗人并没有以通常的"child"或"kid"等词来指称"孩子",而是用了"babe"这个词。这个孩子,还只是个婴儿,或许刚刚开始牙牙学语,连"爸爸"都叫不清楚;或许正在蹒跚学步,摇摇晃晃,还站不稳;或许已经会叫爸爸,会像个小鸭子似的扭过去,叫爸爸抱抱……可是,爸爸,爸爸,你在哪儿呢?诗人叫孩子不要哭,给孩子讲战场上的故事,讲爸爸是个英雄,讲战争是仁慈的,讲战神是伟大的。可怜的孩子,他能否听懂?或许,反而哭得更厉害了。乖啊,不哭,宝贝儿!可是,面对孩子,即使战争再仁慈,即使身死疆场再荣耀,又有什么用呢?能让孩子破涕为笑吗?

最后一节,诗人的镜头转向了母亲。战争是仁慈的,相对于战场上那么多找不到尸首的人来说,这位已经算是很幸运的了!战争是仁慈的,你看,那裹尸布上,战士的胸章还在闪闪发光!诗人接连用了"bright"和"splendid"来形容"shroud",不能不说是一种莫大的讽刺。可是,母亲的心却是谦逊的、卑微的,老母亲不指望儿子能有多大的出息,像全天下的母亲一样,她只希望自己的孩子能够平平安安、健健康康,这就够了。白发人送黑发人的痛苦又有几人能体会?战争是仁慈的吗?战争真的是仁慈的吗?母亲脸上的泪水已经说明了一切,无需多言。

　　整首诗通过三幅立体的画面,全景式地展示了战争给士兵及其亲人所带来的巨大伤痛,表达出诗人对战争的深恶痛绝和强烈愤慨。诗中反复出现的"Do not weep. /War is kind."以及"These men were born to drill and die"等是反讽手法的极致体现,把情感的宣泄一再推向高潮。此外,这首诗歌中意象的构建(集中了视觉、听觉和触觉的意象)以及一些颜色词(如 blazing, red, gold, bright)的运用也独具特色,符合克莱恩印象主义的创作风格。总体而言,《战争是仁慈的》不愧是战争诗中的翘楚。

3. Suicide in the Trenches[①]

Siegfried Sassoon

I knew a simple soldier boy
Who grinned at life in empty joy,
Slept soundly through the lonesome dark,
And whistled early with the lark.

In winter trenches[②], cowed[③] and glum,
With crumps[④] and lice and lack of rum[⑤],
He put a bullet through his brain.
No one spoke of him again.

You smug-faced crowds with kindling eye
Who cheer when soldier lads march by,

Sneak home and pray you'll never know
The hell where youth and laughter go.

【诗人简介】西格弗里德·沙逊（Siegfried Sassoon，1886—1967），沙逊家族成员，20世纪英国著名诗人、传记作家和反战人士。

【注释】

① 此诗是英国诗人西格弗里德·沙逊根据自己在第一次世界大战中的亲身经历写成，收录于1918年出版的诗集《反攻及其他诗歌》(*Counter-Attack and Other Poems*)

② trench：战壕。

③ cowed：吓倒的，受惊吓的。

④ crump：炸弹爆裂声。

⑤ rum：朗姆酒。在战场上，英国军队有时会给士兵喝酒以鼓舞士气。

【作品赏析】

西格弗里德·沙逊既是诗人、作家，更是一名在战场上厮杀的士兵。他是第一次世界大战的亲历者，曾被派往英国以外的多个地区参战，曾经数次受伤和染上战壕热（trench fever），等，也曾经因为勇猛而获得了"疯杰克（Mad Jack）"的称号和十字军勋章的荣誉。读他的战争诗，绝对会有不一样的感受。

这首《战壕里的自杀》是沙逊的代表作之一，讲述了一个原本单纯快乐的年轻人因为害怕战争而亲手结束自己生命的悲剧故事，折射出诗人对战争一贯的批判态度。全篇由3个四行诗

(quatrain)组成的小节构成,采用抑扬格四音步,韵律为 aabb, ccdd, eeff。作品采用白描的手法,用词朴素简洁,整体的节奏不疾不徐,调子舒缓平和克制,似乎只是在叙述一个普通事件。但是,在看似波澜不惊的表象之下,揭示的却是沉重和发人深省的残酷事实:一个稚气未脱、刚到前线的新兵,在战壕周边隆隆的炮火中饮弹自尽了。这究竟是谁之过?

第一小节中,诗人以生活化的语汇向我们展示了一个大孩子的形象:简单、天真、咧着嘴笑、无忧无虑,除了快乐,再没其他。黑漆漆的夜里,他呼呼大睡,不懂夜的孤独与寂寞。一大清早,他快乐的哨声伴着云雀一起飞向高空。请注意,诗人在这里连续运用了几个成功的修辞手段:押头韵(simple soldier, slept soundly)、比喻(grinned at life in empty joy)和拟声(whistled early with the lark)。

不过,第二小节的开头,迅即出现了灰暗阴冷的背景:战壕,而且是冬天的战壕。这个尚未品尝到生活欢愉的士兵开始害怕,开始担忧,闷闷不乐,失去了笑声。包围他的只有震耳欲聋的枪炮声、烦人的虱子,还有所剩不多的几滴朗姆酒。酒或许可以抵挡一下严冬的酷寒,暖暖身子,可是真的快没有了。接着,毫无征兆地,一声枪响,一颗子弹穿过了他的头颅。就这样,一条生命倏忽逝去,从此再也没有人提起他的名字。在这个小节,第一行的几个修饰词 winter, cowed 和 glum 以及第二行中并列的三个名词 crumps, lice 和 rum 具有极强的震撼力。

显然,第一节和第二节形成了鲜明的对比,原本快乐无忧的孩子理应继续享受他这个年龄应有的快乐,可是他怎么会来到战壕,或许是被硬生生拉去军队,可怜的孩子压根不知道战争的厉害所在,他只是本能地感到压抑与恐惧。无限绝望之中,他用枪结束了自己的生命。或许他只是想要原来的自由,可是枪响过后,一切都化为乌有。生命消失了,何谈自由?战争的恐惧是如此之大,以至于让孩子忘了死亡的恐怖!

第三节,诗人将视角转向了路边欢呼的人群。当目睹那些从战场归来的士兵列队经过时,他们兴奋异常,眼睛里闪着火一样热情的光。可是,诗人却奉劝这些人,赶快回去祈祷吧,祈祷自己永远也不要知道那些年轻的生命、那些无邪的笑声都去了哪里。

如果说前两节是正面描写战争的恐惧,写一个年轻士兵的自杀,那么,最后一节,则可以被看作是对战争恐怖的侧面烘托,写了一群人在战争中的命运,或许比那位年轻士兵更可悲可怜。

总体来看,在这首诗中,诗人似乎在刻意压抑着自己的愤怒,才以异乎寻常的平静语气将一个士兵的自杀娓娓道来,将战争的残酷以及对战争的恐惧娓娓道来,但是细细品味,读者将会觉察到文字背后那种激愤的心情。

4. Sonnet XVIII[①]

Wystan Hugh Auden

Far from the heart of culture[②] he was used:
Abandoned by his general and his lice[③],
Under a padded quilt he closed his eyes
And vanished. He will not be introduced
When this campaign is tidied into books:
No vital knowledge perished in his skull[④];
His jokes were stale; like wartime, he was dull;

His name is lost for ever like his looks.
He neither knew nor chose the Good, but taught us,
And added meaning like a comma, when
He turned to dust in China that our daughters
Be fit to love the earth, and not again
Disgraced before the dogs; that, where are waters,
Mountains and houses, may be also men.

【诗人简介】威斯坦·休·奥登（Wystan Hugh Auden, 1907—1973），英裔美国诗人，被公认为是继托马斯·艾略特之后英语诗坛的代表性人物之一。他周游列国，眼界高远，作品主题深厚，擅长以不同体裁进行创作，对后世影响较大。

【注释】

① 此诗由奥登根据1938年访问战时中国的经历创作而成，收录于1939年出版的散文、诗歌和游记合集《战地行》(*Journey to a War*)。后来，奥登对合集中的诗歌进行修改增删，重新出版了诗集《中国十四行诗》(*Sonnets from China*)，本篇为其中第18首作品，又名《中国兵士》(*Chinese Soldier*)。

② the heart of culture：此处泛指西方。奥登是英国人，从他的角度出发，西方是世界文化的中心，故 Far from the heart of culture 句，意即"在远离西方世界的地方"，换言之，即指"在中国"。

③ his general and his lice：general 意为"将军"，lice 意为"虱子"，把两者并提，看似滑稽，实质上表明了作者对战争的态度。

④ skull：头颅。

【作品赏析】

英裔美国诗人奥登的这首第 18 号十四行诗,是典型的意大利式(也称彼特拉克式)十四行诗,前八行(octave)韵脚为 abbaabba,后六行(sestet)韵脚为 cdcdcd。它是著名的"中国组诗"中的一首,是诗人在抗战期间的中国所见所闻的结果。作品围绕一名不知道名字的中国士兵的死亡,探讨了战争的代价和生命的意义等沉重的话题。不仅如此,作为来自西方世界的一名"旁观者",奥登除了表达对中国抗战的同情和声援以外,还由此阐发开来,对全人类的命运和文明发展提出拷问。也就是说,他不但写中国、写中国人的苦难,同时也把中国的遭遇融合进了世界,把对战时中国的前途和命运的认识及思考置于全人类的大背景之下,反映了诗人高远的境界和深刻的历史意识。

诗歌开篇,我们的眼前呈现出这样一幅场景:在东方的土地上,一名士兵完成了他的使命,此刻已被他的将军所抛弃,连讨厌的虱子都不再理会他。这个可怜人,就着一团破军毯,闭上了眼睛,就这样消失、湮灭。诗人提到,这名士兵简直普通得不能再普通,他的笑话不好笑,整个人就是乏味的代名词,一如战争中难捱的日子。他死了,但他的死并没有使世界损失什么。没有人知道他的名字,更不会记得他的模样。当战场的硝烟散去,荣誉载入史册的时候,仍然不可能有谁想到他。

不过,随后诗人给出了他的赞美之辞。虽然这名死去的士兵默默无闻,平凡得如同一粒沙子,虽然他或许只是出于朴素的想法、甚至是迫于无奈才走上了战场,但他却以自己的无私和献身精神实践了"生得平凡,死得伟大"的崇高境界。他的英勇和壮怀激烈像一个巨大的逗号,为生命注入了新的含义。同时,也正是因为他以及其他千千万万像他一样平凡的人们用生命换来了自由,才使得"我们的女儿得以热爱这人间,不再为狗所凌辱",才使得"有山、有水、有房屋的地方,也能有人烟"。

总之,对中国读者而言,这首诗(还有《中国十四行诗》里面的其他诗作)有它独特的重要性。它不但是优秀的文学作品,具有很高的艺术审美价值,同时也是一段历史的见证,具有划时代的意义。

小 结

战争,不得不说是个沉重的话题。即使是在 21 世纪,战争的暗涌也无处不在。

诗歌,按照一般的理解,大多应该和"浪漫"、"多情"以及"美好"相连。可是,当诗歌遇上战争,就不再是"小桥流水"、"花前月下",而是"铁马冰河"、"家破人亡";不再是"执子之手,与子偕老",而是"土国城漕,我独南行";不再是"青青子衿,悠悠我心",而是"行迈靡靡,中心摇摇"……

战争,意味着"不是你死,就是我死"。像哈代笔下,"我们"本可以是朋友,在路边酒馆小酌或畅饮,本可以"朋友一生一起走,一句话,一辈子,一生情,一杯酒",本可以"雪中送炭,互相帮衬"。可是,不可以!因为有战争,因为必须分出敌我,所以就必须用枪指着对方,拼个你死我活!至于为什么会是这样,为什么非要有战争,为什么非要在战场兵戎相见,为什么非要分出胜负?这些问题,岂是那么容易找到答案的。也许,一开始就是这样,一开始就注定了结局,"我们"没有力量反抗,没有力量改变。战争就是战争,从来如此,没有为什么,也绝不容许有为什么!这就是战争的残酷之处和可怕之处。

战争,意味着"一将功成万骨枯"。像克莱恩笔下,战争是"仁慈的",战争可以让你功成名就,战争可以让你荣归故里,战争的好处很多很多。即使有一天战死沙场,也是为国捐躯,即使和这个世界"挥一挥手,不带走一片云彩",也可以"生的伟大,死的光荣"。如此,反倒不用在人世间受折磨,战争还不够"仁慈"吗?那个姑娘,那个小孩,那个老妇人,还有什么好哭的呢?可是亲爱的,"我"要的不是"你"功成名就,荣归故里,不是"你""生的伟大,死的光荣",不是"你"冰冷地躺在地上一言不发,要的只是"执子之手,与子偕老",要的只是"日出而作,日落而息","你"怎么忍心丢下还在学说话的孩子,怎么忍心老母亲"白发人送黑发人"?

　　战争,意味着"恐惧与死亡"。像沙逊笔下,一个年轻活泼快乐的生命在战争的魔掌下,骤然被碾得粉碎。纵然他对这个世界还有满腔的激情与热情,纵然他对生活还依依不舍,可是,与战争的狰狞与可怖相比,这些激情、热情、期盼又算得了什么呢?"生命诚可贵,爱情价更高,若为自由故,二者皆可抛。"战争,剥夺了自由,活着还有什么意义呢?"不如归去,不如归去……"

　　战争,意味着"我轻轻地来,正如我轻轻地走"。像奥登笔下,一个连名字都没有留下的士兵,他的生命悄然陨落。"没有花香,没有树高,我是一棵无人知道的小草",也许,连小草也比不上吧,小草至少有接受阳光雨露生长的自由。而"我",除了在战场上挥动手中的"杀人工具"外,还能做什么呢?"我"知道自己很可能有一天会像其他兄弟一样,归于尘土,与大地共眠,"我"知道自己很不起眼,渺小得如同一粒沙子,"我"知道自己的力量远不足以杀死所有的敌人,保家卫国,可是,"我"仍然会用全力,哪怕付出自己的生命,为了这些山、这些水、这些人!

　　……

　　翻阅英美诗歌历史,关于战争的诗篇可以说数不胜数。不过,通过上述四首经过我们精心挑选的作品，相信读者必定对此已有了一个基本的了解和认识。亚伯拉罕·林肯曾经说过，"战争没有任何好处，除了它的结束。"（There is nothing good in war, except its ending.）所以，如果我们不能完全消除战争，那就祈祷战争早一点结束，祈祷战争可以少一点再少一点吧。

扩展阅读篇目

To Lucasta , on Going to the Wars by Richard Lovelace

The Charge of the Light Brigade by Lord Alfred Tennyson

A Wife in London by Thomas Hardy

A Meditation in Time of War by William Butler Yeats

The Recruit by A. E. Housman

The Unreturning by Wilfred Owen

Anthem for Doomed Youth by Wilfred Owen

A Ballad of Footmen by Amy Lowell

The Death of the Ball Turret Gunner by Randall Jarrell

Country at War by Robert Graves

I Have a Rendezvous with Death by Alan Seeger

Ode to the Confederate Dead by Allen Tate

For the Union Dead by Robert Lowell

form
第四章

诗歌与死亡

点 题

One short sleep past, we wake eternally,
And death shall be no more; Death, thou shalt die.
——From *Holy Sonnet X*: *Death*, *Be Not Proud* by John Donne

死亡,是每个人所必须要面对的,它既神秘又普通至极。按照中国人的传统观念,生老病死,这些都是人生道路上的不同阶段,既有生,就必然会有死。古往今来,无论中西、死亡,都是诗人笔下恒久关注的主题。他们有的侧重描写具体的死亡场景,借以突出死亡可怖、神秘和不可预知的一面;有的专注于对逝者的追忆和缅怀之中,由此发出生命短暂的哀叹或珍惜当下的吁请;还有的则更加冷静深刻,他们不拘泥于具体的死亡事件或情节,站在超脱死亡的抽象层面上,或意图穷极死亡的本质和意义,或着眼于探讨生与死的辩证关系,等等。总之,凡涉及死亡题材的诗歌,往往寄托着作者对生存与死亡等问题的困惑不安与思考,同时也表达了他们形形色色的人生观和死亡观。当然,由于中西方历史、文化、宗教等方面的差异,诗人们在对待死亡的问题上,也会展现出不尽相同的态度。中国诗人受儒家思想的影响,多希望在有生之年能闯出

第四章
诗歌与死亡

一番事业、光宗耀祖。他们对人死以后的情形不太感兴趣,甚至不相信人死后有"灵魂升天"一说,因而,诗中抒写的大多是生死离别或面对死亡的无助和无奈,作品偏于感性的成分多一些,但是,对于死亡的哲学意义上的深究就显得不足。与此形成鲜明对照的是,同样面对死亡这个命题,英美诗人一般更倾向于理性的思考。他们固然也会渲染死亡的残忍与恐怖,也时常悲叹生命的倏忽无常和死亡的无可避免,但悲天悯人之余,他们仍不忘发出对死亡的追问和拷问。而且,从另一个角度来看,英美诗人虽然写的是死亡,却每每能够保持一份平静祥和、豁达开朗的心绪,一些诗人甚至达到了超脱的境界。比如,美国女诗人萨拉·蒂斯代尔(Sara Teasdale)曾写过一首题为"如果死亡是善良的"的诗。在这首诗中,"死亡"一点也不见恐怖和狰狞的面目,反倒显得十分"善良",与"生"也并没有那么严格的界限。再比如,英国诗人约翰·多恩(John Donne)那首著名的"神圣十四行诗",其直面死亡、挑战死亡和视死如归的气度,以及字里行间所透出来的精神力量,确实令读者心灵为之一震。如果要就英美死亡主题的诗歌作一个简单分析、归纳的话,我们认为,它主要体现出如下一些特点:

首先,它与主导西方人精神生活的宗教(特别是基督教)有着很深的渊源。基督教认为,人有两种生命,即身体的生命和灵性的生命;同时,人也有两种死亡,即身体的死亡和灵性的死亡。在西方人的认知里,"原罪——赎罪——死亡——永生"的宗教观已深深地渗入他们的潜意识之中。从《旧约》中的原罪意识延伸出来的对于死亡的坦然,到《新约》中把死亡当作一种希望,标志着永生的开始。简单地说,基督教认为人死后是一个全新的世界,所以,他们往往轻视现世,而向往超验的后世。在他们看来,人生来即有原罪,现实世界(现世)是一个充满罪恶和痛苦的世界,而死后升入天堂,得到来自上帝的爱,并与主真正永久地在一起才是他们的最终归属。因此,无论对于普通社会成员,还是对于作家诗人而言,死亡并不是什么可怕的事情,相反,甚至还抱有某种期待。因为,死亡并不意味着结束,而是重生。正是基于这种西方人独特的死亡观,多少年来,英美诗坛与死亡相关的佳作名篇才呈现出别具特色的魅力。比如,在莎士比亚笔下,死亡被看成是对痛苦人生的一种解脱;在狄金森笔下,死亡成为一道惬意的风景,是如花少女幻想的幸福终点;在丁尼生笔下,死亡既庄重又朴素,却没有一丝悲伤和不舍。

其次,作品的内容虽然离不开死亡,但真正的重点却在阐述人"生"的道理。生与死,或者,死与生,是一对既对立又统一的矛盾体,对于宗教意识浓厚的西方社会更是如此。就诗人而言,对死亡的探究,实际上就是从另外一个层面展示对生存意义的思考。作为生命的终结,死亡固然让人感到恐惧,但是,死亡之于生命又不是毫无意义的,它可以使生命的价值得以澄明。死亡,是启迪生命和激发生命的力量,没有死亡的黑暗,也就见证不到生命的灿烂。英国浪漫主义诗人济慈在现实生活中曾多次眼睁睁地看着死亡降临在自己的亲朋好友身上,他经历了死亡带来的痛苦,也感受到了死亡的残忍与决绝,正因为如此,他才更加体会到"生"的意义所在。特别是,当后来诗人预感到自己也即将面临死亡的时候,他反而能以一种从容淡定的态度,以一种赞赏的目光看遍大自然的美景,由此实践了他珍惜人"生"的愿望。美国浪漫主义诗人埃德加·爱伦·坡是一位天生的怪才,他以擅长书写恐怖的死亡以及另类的美而得名。在他的作品里,即便是死亡,也往往美得令人心碎。他的《乌鸦》(*The Raven*)、《致海伦》(*To Helen*)和《安娜贝尔·李》(*Annabel Lee*)等都是典型的例子。对他来说,死亡不只是他钟情的主题,更是他表达对生命的热爱与追求的有效手段。

第三,在相当程度上,这类诗歌也具备抒发人伦亲情的功能。在死亡主题的诗歌中,悼亡诗是比较常见的一种,也是最能触动人心弦的书写形式。这类诗歌或为痛失爱侣而悲痛洒泪,或因亲人撒手人寰而伤心哀恸,或因挚友的猝然离世而扼腕慨叹。此时,死亡成了诗意的凶手,诗人们唯有将情感极力宣泄于笔端,才能真正告慰失去至亲挚友的诗人,告慰亡者的灵魂。英国维多利亚时期的伟大诗人丁尼生为怀念亡友亚瑟·哈勒姆曾经创作了长篇组诗《悼念集》(In Memoriam A. H. H.),寄托了诗人无限的哀思。爱伦·坡的名作《安娜贝尔·李》是诗人为悼念他的亡妻而作,诗中唯美的意境衬托出的淡淡哀愁恰到好处地表达了两人之间矢志不渝的爱情。弥尔顿(John Milton)为悼念他第二任妻子凯瑟琳·伍德柯克,也曾写下过千古绝唱《梦亡妻》(On His Deceased Wife)。

总之,在诗人眼里,死亡并不是生命的结束,而是生命真正的开始。同时,死亡也从另一个角度让人们更加看清楚生命和生活的本质,从而更加懂得如何珍惜生命、珍惜亲人的爱和朋友的友谊,珍爱身边的一草一木。本章收录了狄金森、丁尼生、济慈和莎士比亚四位英美著名诗人的代表作各一首,通过对这些作品必要的分析和恰当的点评,有助于读者对"诗歌"与"死亡"之间的关系有一个初步的认识。

名篇导读

1. Because I could not stop for Death① —
Emily Dickinson

Because I could not stop for Death —

He kindly stopped for me —
The Carriage held but just Ourselves —
And Immortality.

We slowly drove — He knew no haste
And I had put away
My labor and my leisure too,
For His Civility② —

We passed the School, where Children strove
At Recess③ — in the Ring —
We passed the Fields of Gazing Grain —
We passed the Setting Sun —

Or rather — He passed Us —
The Dews drew quivering and chill —
For only Gossamer④, my Gown —
My Tippet⑤ — only Tulle⑥ —

We paused before a House that seemed
A Swelling of the Ground⑦ —
The Roof was scarcely visible —
The Cornice⑧ — in the Ground —

Since then — 'tis⑨ Centuries — and yet
Feels shorter than the Day

第四章
诗歌与死亡

I first surmised the Horses' Heads

Were toward Eternity —

【注释】

① 此诗首次刊印于 1890 年出版的《诗歌集：第一辑》(*Poems, Series 1*)，该诗集由艾米莉·狄金森(Emily Dickinson,1830—1886)生前好友 Mabel Loomis Todd 和 Thomas Wentworth Higginson 协助整理编辑出版。当时,该诗的标题是"The Chariot"。在 1955 年由 Thomas H. Johnson 编辑出版的集注版狄金森诗集中,该诗被标为第 712 号作品。

② His Civility：此处喻指死神文质彬彬、殷勤有礼。

③ Recess：课间休息。

④ Gossamer：精细织物；薄纱；薄如蝉翼的衣服。

⑤ Tippet：女式披肩。

⑥ Tulle：薄纱。

⑦ Swelling of the Ground：本意为"地上凸起或隆起的部分",此处指"坟墓"或"墓地"。

⑧ Cornice：檐口；檐板；飞檐；楣。

⑨ 'tis：相当于 it is,多见于诗歌中。

【作品赏析】

"死亡"是诗歌永恒的主题,在艾米莉·狄金森的笔下也不例外。这位 19 世纪美国最重要的女诗人一生创作颇丰,其中与"死亡"这一主题直接相关的就有约六百首。选录在此的这首 *Because I could not stop for Death* 是狄金森最负盛名、最具代表性的"死亡"诗。

在这首诗中,诗人以平和、克制、舒缓的语调娓娓道来,为读者讲述了发生在"我"和死亡之间的奇特故事。不过,作品虽然以死亡作为主线贯穿始终,我们却看不见、也闻不到与死亡如影随形的压抑、恐怖和凄惨的成分。诗人巧妙地运用了拟人化的手法,将"我"化身成一个天真少女,被"死亡"这位彬彬有礼的绅士所深深打动,因而甘愿停止劳作,放弃闲暇时光,坐上象征着灵车的死亡马车。在同座"永生"的陪伴下,"我"穿越课间休息的小学校,路过长满庄稼的田地,不知不觉到达了目的地——坟墓。几个世纪飞逝而过,"我"发现自己乘坐的马车已然驶向永生。在诗的第一、二节中,诗人以形象化的语言塑造了别具一格的"死亡"形象,赋予"死亡"诸多人性化的特质。比如,"死亡"竟然会像绅士一般客客气气地停下来等我(He kindly stopped for me),他的举止成熟稳重、彬彬有礼、毫不慌乱(He knew no haste),与一般人印象中的"死亡"形象简直有天壤之别。全诗的第三节是最具有象征意义的部分,三个人("我"、"死亡"和"永生")路过了象征着童年的学校、象征着成年的田地和象征着暮年的日落,这一旅程象征着人类一生的过程。在第四节中,"我"开始有了人活着时候的反应,能感觉到黑暗与寒冷。比如,诗人写道,"The Dews drew quivering and chill",虽然描写的是露水,但其实表现了人对命运的恐惧感。第五小节描写了"我们"三人停在了一座像房子的建筑前,开始陷入了对死亡的沉思。最后一个小节中,收尾的两行:"I first surmised the Horses' Heads/Were toward Eternity—"乃点睛之笔,表明"我"明白了人生追求的最高境界是"永生",只有死后的"永生"才能解决现世的困境,这也是全诗最富有哲理的启示。

从创作技巧来看,这是典型的狄金森式的作品。整首诗短小、精炼,但内容十分丰厚。诗中的抑扬格四音步与抑扬格三音步相间，取得了独特的音乐美。不仅如此，一些传统手法的妙用，如行内押韵（slowly drove; my labor and my leisure）和头韵（At Recess — in the Ring; Gazing Grain）等也使得它读起来更加琅琅上口。此外，单词首字母大写也是狄金森惯常使用的一种手段。在这首诗歌中，有不少这样的例子。最后，全诗出现了多达22处破折号，或用在句中，或用在句尾，起到了突出、解释、强化或省略的作用。这也是狄金森诗歌的一大标志。

2. Crossing the Bar①
Alfred, Lord Tennyson

Sunset and evening star,
    And one clear call for me!
And may there be no moaning② of the bar,
    When I put out to sea.

But such a tide as moving seems asleep,
    Too full for sound and foam③,
When that which drew from out the boundless deep
    Turns again home.

Twilight and evening bell,
    And after that the dark!
And may there be no sadness of farewell,
    When I embark④;

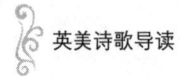

  For tho' from out our bourne of Time and Place⑤
    The flood may bear me far,
  I hope to see my Pilot⑥ face to face
    When I have crost⑦ the bar.

【诗人简介】阿尔弗雷德·丁尼生爵士(Alfred, Lord Tennyson, 1809—1892),继华兹华斯之后的英国桂冠诗人。诗作题材广泛、想象丰富、辞藻绮丽、音调铿锵,其131首的组诗《悼念》被视为英国文学史上最优秀的哀歌之一。

【注释】
  ① 此诗由1850年获英国桂冠诗人称号的阿尔弗雷德·丁尼生爵士于1889年创作,选自其作品集《悼念集》。标题中的Bar,应作"沙洲"解,所谓"过沙洲",在这里是一种比喻的用法,含有"走向死亡"的意思。
  ② moaning:指大海拍击港口的沙洲时发出的类似呻吟的声音。
  ③ Too full for sound and foam:潮涨得太满,以至于大海似乎悄无声息,看不见一点泡沫。
  ④ embark:上船。
  ⑤ For tho' from out our bourne of Time and Place:在这里,tho'是though的缩写;bourne相当于boundary或limit。
  ⑥ Pilot:原意为"领航员",此处喻指"上帝"。
  ⑦ crost:相当于crossed。

【作品赏析】
  《过沙洲》是丁尼生年届八旬时所作的一首诗,据说,当时仅用时10分钟即一挥而就,并且成为诗人晚年最重要的作品之一。一般认为,此诗抒发了死亡逼近时诗人乐天知命的襟怀,暗示了其对死亡所持的豁达和超然的态度。

这首诗歌有几个突出的特点:首先,象征手法的妙用。诗歌的标题"Crossing the Bar"即具有强烈的象征意义。Bar 在这里可以解读为生与死的分界线,而 Cross 一词则具有双重象征意义:它既有"十字架"的意思,象征传统的基督教思想,因为耶稣就是在十字架上被绞死的,同时也有"穿越"和"跨越"的意思。因此,所谓 Crossing the Bar,实际上喻指诗人即将跨越生死边界,走入另一个世界。此外,在第四小节的第一行中,Time and Place 采用了首字母大写的形式,因为诗人要强调这里是时空的终点,象征着诗人即将到达的永恒之地。在这一节的第三行中,同样首字母大写的 Pilot 一词,原意为"海上航行的领航员",但是,显然在这里它被用来指称上帝。正如娴熟的领航员可以引导船只安然渡过沙洲一样,在诗人看来,上帝也必然会引导他平静地渡过险恶的死亡浅滩,由此表达出他对上帝的笃信以及对即将到来的死亡的坦然。第二,是丰富的视觉和听觉效果的构建。这首诗的主题是老年和死亡,为了烘托气氛、强化主题,诗人营造了一幅夕阳西下之时大海静谧无声、一位老者独自向着大海深处远行的画面。他选用了一些看似平淡无奇的单词,比如,第一小节中的 sunset and evening star 以及 call 和 moaning 等,但是,这些词汇却构成了强烈的视觉和听觉上的冲击。再比如,第二小节第二行中的 sound and foam 则兼具了视觉和听觉的双重效果。类似的例子还包括 bar, tide, boundless deep, twilight, dark 等,这些词汇的选择使读者产生身临其境的感觉。第三,是诗行长短相间的独到设计。这首诗共包括 4 个小节,每节四行(由四个诗行构成的小节被称为四行诗节 quatrain），押韵格式基本为 abab。在每个小节中，尽管每行的长度不一，但基本上第一、三行要比第二、四行长，这就好比大海中交替起伏的波浪，敲击着诗人的心，也抓住了读者的注意力。

总体而言，整首诗在描述的过程中，诗人始终以一种平和沉稳的心态，把走向死亡之路时的心情抒写得犹如回家一般。一首死亡诗却不见一丝恐怖和悲伤，反而让人感到某种静谧的人与自然的和谐之美，还能净化和提升人的灵魂，不愧是一首绝佳好诗。人既然是自然万物的一部分，生生死死，就应该顺其自然，所以人的生死与花开花落的自然现象其实并无多大差异。作为华兹华斯之后英国的又一位桂冠诗人，丁尼生的作品在当时曾深受读者欢迎，这首《过沙洲》即是有力的佐证。

3. When I Have Fears[①]

John Keats

When I have fears that I may cease to be
   Before my pen has glean'd[②] my teeming brain[③],
Before high-piled books, in charactery[④],
   Hold like rich garners[⑤] the full ripen'd grain;
When I behold, upon the night's starr'd face,
   Huge cloudy symbols of a high romance,
And think that I may never live to trace
   Their shadows, with the magic hand of chance;
And when I feel, fair creature of an hour[⑥],
   That I shall never look upon thee more,

Never have relish in the faery power⑦
　　Of unreflecting love;— then on the shore
Of the wide world I stand alone, and think
Till love and fame to nothingness do sink.

【诗人简介】 约翰•济慈(John Keats, 1795—1821),英国诗人,欧洲浪漫主义运动的杰出代表,与雪莱、拜伦齐名。主要作品有《伊莎贝拉》、《海伯利安》、《夜莺颂》、《希腊古瓮颂》等。

【注释】

① 此诗最初见于济慈 1818 年 1 月 31 日写给友人雷诺兹(J. H. Reynolds)的一封信中。不过,诗人在世时,此诗从未发表。直到 1848 年,它才首次刊印于米尔恩(Richard Monckton Milnes)写的一本济慈传记里,并逐渐为人所知晓,被认为是他最成功的作品之一。

② glean'd: gleaned 的简略形式,是动词 glean 的过去式,意即"拾(落穗);收集(资料)"。第四行和第五行中的 ripen'd 和 starr'd 也分别相当于 ripened 和 starred。

③ teeming brain: 意即"大量的;充盈的;汹涌澎湃的;拥挤的"。

④ charactery: 意即"表达思想的文字或符号"。

⑤ garner: 相当于 granary, grain storehouse,意即"谷仓"。

⑥ fair creature of an hour: fair creature 指"美丽的女子"、"美人",此处可理解为指代"爱情",所谓 fair creature of an hour 则是一种夸张的说法,意思是说"爱情转瞬即已逝去"。

⑦ faery power: faery 相当于 fairy;所谓 faery power 此处指"(爱情)神奇的魔力"。

【作品赏析】

约翰·济慈是英国浪漫主义诗歌的杰出代表,他虽然26岁即早逝,但诗才横溢,成就与拜伦、雪莱齐名。济慈擅长表现景物的色彩感和立体感,语言风格华丽,所写的颂歌(ode)尤其出色。他在《希腊古瓮颂》里曾提出"美即是真,真即是美"的主张,对后世的文论创作影响巨大。

这首《每当我害怕》作于1818年,是在诗人及其家人陷入一系列困境、面临生死考验的背景下写成的。当时,济慈的弟弟正因肺结核住院,而济慈本人的身体状况也不容乐观。诗歌采用莎士比亚十四行诗(也称伊丽莎白或英国式十四行诗)(Shakespearean or Elizabethan or English Sonnet)的形式,韵式为标准的abab cdcd efef gg。与典型的莎士比亚十四行诗一样,这首诗歌也可分为三个四行诗节(quatrain)和结尾的对句(concluding couplet)。其中,前面的三个四行诗节分别以"每当我害怕……"、"每当我看见……"和"每当我感觉……"起始,层次清晰,情感表达一步步得到升华。在第一个四行诗节中,令诗人唏嘘不已的是生命苦短,对艺术的追求却不得不戛然而止。他纵然如何迫切地想要创作出华丽的诗章、成就一番伟业,但是,偏偏命运弄人,天不遂人愿。在这里,诗人运用丰富的想象将他想要做出一番成就的渴望刻画得淋漓尽致,例如,他想象丰收的情景,丰收代表着收获,而饱满的谷子则象征着有价值的创作。在第二个四行诗节中,诗人把目光转向了更为广阔的自然天地。他看到了缀满星星的夜空,还看到了翻滚起伏、令人浮想联翩的云朵。他由此生出了无尽的遗憾:他是多么希望能够追随白云、攀上苍穹,为大自然的美景写下一曲曲赞歌。在第三个四行诗节中,诗人谈到了爱情。他把亲密的爱人比喻成 fair creature of an hour,写出了因爱情转瞬即逝或不易获得而产生的苦恼。但是,他显然仍渴望无忧无虑的爱情,相信爱情的魔力,因为他随后即写下了 the faery power of unreflecting love 的诗句。值得注意的细节是,与前两个部分相比,这一小节显得稍短。这似乎暗示了诗人在现实中虽然渴望获得恋人的爱,但却无力享受。结尾的对句当然是全篇的高潮,诗人设计了一个独特的场景:开阔、广袤的世界边缘,"我"独自一人,沉思良久,终于悟出了困扰心底的难题的答案:所谓名誉和爱情,到头来终究都会化为乌有。

总之,济慈的这首《每当我害怕》给人的感觉是包裹着淡淡的忧伤,它涉及死亡这个题材,揭示了死亡即丧失,包括丧失爱情、名誉,甚至永恒。不过,也有人认为,这首诗歌并不完全是伤感的。因为正如诗歌最后所提示的,当诗人看透了生命的玄机、看破了一切,他便不必再感到愤怒、绝望和无助,他反而获得了解脱。从这个意义上来说,它可以被看作是一首具有深刻哲理内涵的"死亡"诗。

4. Sonnet 73[①]

William Shakespeare

That time of year thou[②] mayst[③] in me behold[④]
When yellow leaves, or none, or few, do hang
Upon those boughs which shake against the cold,
Bare ruined choirs[⑤], where late[⑥] the sweet birds sang.
In me thou see'st the twilight of such day
As after sunset fadeth[⑦] in the west;
Which by and by black night doth take away,
Death's second self, that seals up all in rest.

In me thou see'st the glowing of such fire,
That on the ashes of his youth doth lie,
As the death-bed, whereon⑧ it must expire,
Consum'd⑨ with that which it was nourish'd by.
This thou perceiv'st, which makes thy love more strong,
To love that well, which thou must leave ere long⑩.

【诗人简介】威廉·莎士比亚(William Shakespeare,1564—1616),英国文艺复兴时期伟大的诗人、剧作家,同时也被公认为是英国文学史和世界文坛最著名的作家之一,一生共创作154首十四行诗、2首长叙事诗和37部戏剧。

【注释】

① 此诗选自莎士比亚154首十四行诗中的第73首。原诗没有标题,一般习惯将其第一行 That time of year thou mayst in me behold 用作标题。

② thou:Elizabethan English,相当于 you,是主格。第十三行中的 thy,则相当于 you 的所有格,即 your。

③ mayst:相当于 may。此后出现的 see'st 和 perceiv'st 也分别相当于 see 和 perceive。

④ behold:多出现在诗歌中,相当于 see。

⑤ Bare ruined choirs:意即"几乎荒废的唱诗坛"。

⑥ late:相当于 lately。

⑦ fadeth:相当于 fades。此后出现的 doth 也相当于 does。

⑧ whereon:相当于 on which。

⑨ Consum'd:相当于 consumed。此后出现的 nourish'd 也

相当于 nourished。

⑩ ere long：相当于 before long。

【作品赏析】

威廉·莎士比亚是英语文学中永恒的经典,他不但是伟大的剧作家,同时也是第一流的诗人,他的十四行诗代表着诗歌创作的最高境界。他一生共创作了 154 首十四行诗,这里选录的是其中的第 73 首。这首诗歌以其严谨的结构、生动的语言和丰富的意象给读者留下了深刻的印象。它既是一曲生命的挽歌,同时也是一段爱的颂歌。全诗不仅有对衰老和死亡的恐惧和哀叹,更反映出诗人对生命的炽烈情感。诗歌所传达的信息是:"我"感到自己已进入暮年,不久就要和爱人永别,因此希望在"我"离开人世之前,爱人能好好地、热烈地爱着"我"。

全诗由三节四行诗和结尾的对句组成,韵脚交替进行,抑扬格五音步写成,韵式为 abab, cdcd, efef, gg。前三节四行诗的首句中,诗人以基本相同的句式——That time of year thou mayst in me behold(第一行),In me thou see'st the twilight of such day (第五行)和 In me thou see'st the glowing of such fire(第九行)——来告诉读者自己已是一个风烛残年的老人,并且将不久于人世,从而唤起读者的同情和爱。在这个部分,诗人连续运用了三个比喻。首先,他将"我"目前的生命阶段比作晚秋,也就是树叶凋零、秋风萧瑟的季节。所谓 When yellow leaves, or none, or few, do hang/Upon those boughs which shake against the cold,所谓 Bare ruined choirs, where late the sweet birds sang 等所描绘的即是那种繁华退净之后的荒芜景象,触发了很多惆怅。其次,诗人将"我"比喻成日落后的黄昏,那是夜色将至、夕阳的余晖即将消失而被黑暗所替代的时刻。请注意,诗人在这里甚至把黑夜比喻为"死神的第二个自我,把一切悄悄地收入囊中"。可见,在诗人的眼里,"黄昏——黑夜——死亡"的线条已赫然在目。第三个四行诗节中,诗人则将"我"比作即将熄灭的火苗,这个比喻与之前的秋天和黄昏的意象有所不同。秋天过后是冬天,冬天过后是春天,生命仍然会复苏。黄昏虽然来临,可黑夜过后依然还有白昼,生命的希望还在。但是,火苗一旦熄灭,就无法再继续燃烧,这似乎在暗示青春一去永不复返。总体来说,这三个小节的基调感时伤怀,给人以一种暮气沉沉、萧条肃杀的感觉。不过,在随后收尾的两行,诗人笔锋一转,却发出了另一种的声音。他写道:"This thou perceiv'st, which makes thy love more strong,/To love that well, which thou must leave ere long(你看出这一点,也就使你的爱更坚强,/好好地爱你不久要离开的对象。)"由此,读者才真正体会到诗人写作的深意,他并非只是在悲叹青春的易逝,相反,他更多地是在表达对生命和爱的渴望以及赞美。

莎士比亚的十四行诗主题多与爱情有关,其中的第 71—74 首则被认为是一个死亡随想的系列。不过很显然,即便是探讨死亡的话题,诗人也没有忘记把它和爱以及人生置于同一个背景之下,这就是大诗人的不同寻常之处。

小 结

死亡,是一个敏感的话题,却也是一个谁也无法回避的话题。谈及死亡,普通人的反应不外乎忧虑、恐惧、战战兢兢或听天由命。因为死亡意味着生命的终结,意味着离别,意味着对亲人致命的打击。不过,在诗人的眼里,死亡显然包含了更多的含义。

狄金森可以说是一位"死亡艺术家",她在长年蜗居的生活状

第四章
诗歌与死亡

态下,把自己沉入生与死的边界,反复地咀嚼死亡的意味、体察死亡的感觉。她的那些关于死亡的诗歌一方面是她长期冥思玄想的结果,同时也从一个侧面反映了她所处时代之中社会和思想的冲突。她不是单纯地描写死亡,也不满足于简单地歌唱或诅咒死亡;换言之,她并没有把死亡仅仅当作诗歌的素材来对待。她所做的是在探讨和界定死亡的前提下,表明自己的态度。她不认为死亡有多么可怕,相反,死亡还可以成就凤凰涅槃式的重生或永生,因为死亡是通往重生或永生的必由之路。对狄金森来说,"生"、"死"和"永生"成了她一生孜孜以求的哲学问题。与狄金森一样,丁尼生也是一位赋予死亡别样含义的伟大诗人。如果说狄金森对于死亡的理解多来自苦苦的思索,那么,丁尼生的死亡解读则更多基于他自身的生活经历,更具有真切感。他在写《过沙洲》时已达八十高龄,而且,据说这首诗的写作还和他此前的一次海上经历有关。因此,他的那种面对死亡坦然自若的姿态,自然令人生出别样的肃然起敬的心情。济慈是一位史所罕见的奇才,他不常写死亡,他的诗歌以歌咏生命、吟唱大自然的"真"和"美"居多。他的《夜莺颂》(*Ode to a Nightingale*)、《希腊古瓮颂》(*Ode on a Grcian Urn*)、《致秋天》(*To Autumn*)和《蝈蝈与蛐蛐》(*On the Grasshopper and Cricket*)等足可证明。《每当我害怕》是一个例外,在这首诗歌中,济慈在亲人遭遇不幸、面临死亡威胁的情形下,想到了自己的前途和命运。诗中有真性情的流露,也不乏伤感和悲戚的成分,不过,即便如此,诗人还是传达出了某种正面和积极的信息。他也许害怕死亡,喟叹生命苦短,但死亡其实并不可怕,真正可怕的是面对死亡的消极退缩,可怕的是碌碌无为而死,也正是因为有了这样的胸襟和气魄才使得济慈在短暂的生命里创作出了许多不朽的作品。至于莎士比亚,他的高度和深度已无须赘言。时间、生命、死亡和永恒是莎士比亚十四行诗的主旋律，它们和爱情一起构成了他"不朽"的精神追求。莎士比亚在诗歌创作中探索永恒的可能性，并通过诗歌的创作而获得了文本的永恒。

当然，除了上述几位诗人以外，英美文学史上还有许多书写死亡的高手，他们都在自己的作品中直接或间接地涉及了死亡的主题。比如，与狄金森同时代的英国女诗人罗塞蒂曾写过一首《上坡》(*Uphill*)。在这首诗里，罗塞蒂采取一问一答的形式引出了"生与死"的永恒命题。在她看来，生命恰似一次蜿蜒而上的上坡历程，而在那坡顶，可以让疲惫的旅客歇脚的休憩之所就是死亡。死亡并不神秘，也没有那么可怕，死亡是一件自然而然的事情。因为既然有开始，就注定会有结束。在20世纪50年代和60年代的美国"自白派"诗人中，西尔维亚·普拉斯是一位最热衷于探讨死亡的诗人，她的不少作品，如《拉撒路夫人》(*Lady Lazarus*)、《镜子》(*Mirror*)和《边缘》(*Edge*)等从不同的侧面论及了死亡问题。她最后在英国伦敦自杀身亡，由此也实践了她和死亡之间的约定。诗人们在面对死亡的恐惧时，选择用诗歌来"拯救"自己，以此来确保生命的价值和意义。他们创作的根本动力是对"永生"的追求，而把自己短暂的生命转移或存储到拥有强大生命力的艺术作品中，以此达到对抗死亡、消除恐惧的目的，这是他们反抗死亡威胁的一种方式。生即是死，死即是生，生死之间已无明显的界限，诗人们由此在创作诗歌的过程中实现了自我和灵魂的永恒与不朽。

扩展阅读篇目

Elegy Written in a Country Churchyard by Thomas Gray

Uphill by Christina Gabriel Rossetti

Remembrance by Emily Bronte

第四章
诗歌与死亡

Do Not Go Gentle into That Good Night by Dylan Thomas

An Irish Airman Foresees His Death by William Butler Yeats

The Raven by Edgar Allan Poe

Holy Sonnet X: Death Be Not Proud by John Donne

When Death Comes by Mary Oliver

A Happy Man by Edwin Arlington Robinson

Dream Song 324: An Elegy for W.C.W., the Lovely Man by John Berryman

Edge by Sylvia Plath

The Soldier by Rupert Brook

Tears, Idle Tears by Alfred Lord Tennyson

Funeral Blues by W. H. Auden

第五章

诗歌与城市

点 题

All great art is born of the metropolis.

—— Ezra Pound

城市的出现距今已经有六千年以上的历史。早在公元前3世纪，亚洲西部美索不达米亚地区即出现了世界上最早的城邦国家，由此也掀开了城市文明崭新的一页。城市的发展与繁荣，往往伴随着文学艺术的兴盛。在古代，文学的表达形式主要是诗歌，其涉及的主题或为赞美诸神的圣歌，或为探讨生死的道德说教，也有一些是记载个人命运种种的悲喜剧。这些有着浓厚的神话、宗教色彩的作品虽受益于古代城邦的繁荣和兴盛，但是，它们之中专门描述城市景象和生活的诗篇却少之又少。虽然公元前8世纪左右出现的荷马史诗——《伊利亚特》和《奥德赛》中或多或少有反映希腊城邦的繁华景象的内容，但那也只是为了烘托作品中的英雄形象并为其主题服务的。

中古时期的欧洲文学以英雄主义与骑士传统为特色，与古代的文学一样，鲜见有专门描述城市景象的诗歌作品。这一时期重要的文学成果来自阿拉伯文学的《一千零一夜》。《一千零一夜》被

第五章
诗歌与城市

认为是当时阿拉伯社会生活的一部百科全书,全景式地展示了当时社会的世态人情。其中很多故事涉及国王、大臣、市民等主题,也在一定程度上反映了当时的城市生活景象。但是《一千零一夜》并不是严格意义上的诗歌集,其表现手法多为诗文并茂,主要以日常口语为主,辅以故事人物的吟唱,因此,这一时期单纯表现城市生活的诗歌较为少见。

近代以来,由于文艺复兴运动、宗教改革以及18世纪接踵而至的启蒙运动,欧洲文学迎来了一个活跃时期。意大利文学出现了薄伽丘的《十日谈》,法国文坛出现了拉伯雷的《巨人传》,西班牙则涌现了塞万提斯的《堂吉诃德》。在英国,宫廷诗歌与市民戏剧也开始变得兴盛起来,出现了乔叟的《坎特伯雷故事集》。这部作品的故事涵盖了当时英国社会各个阶层,其中出现的人物包括骑士、修女、医生、教士、律师等,客观上反映了英国城市生活的面貌。到了16世纪伊丽莎白统治的时期,英国文坛迎来了戏剧上的活跃时期,莎士比亚的戏剧自此闻名于世。在诗歌方面,英国的宫廷诗歌占主导地位,著名的作品有斯宾塞的《仙后》等。但是,宫廷诗歌主要服务于王公贵族,是用来为统治阶级歌功颂德的,因此,还不能归入真正描写城市生活的诗歌类别。

18世纪中叶,以英国人瓦特改良蒸汽机为标志,机器工业开始取代传统的手工业,成为主要的生产方式,工业革命由此向着大规模的方向发展。随着工业革命的发展,城市化进程有了明显的加快。人们的生活水平得到了明显改善,生活方式也发生了诸多的变化。但是,无可回避的是,这种迅速而来的变化也给城市带来了诸多的难题,比如贫富差距、腐败和犯罪等。与此相对应,在文学领域,包括诗歌创作领域,诗人们则敏锐地抓住了这一特殊社会发展时期所呈现的特殊社会风貌。他们深入城市的各个角落,凭着自己的观察和判断，搜寻和梳理独特的、鲜活的、不同于以往的城市生活素材，反映城市各个侧面的、令人印象深刻的作品也开始相继涌现。比如，布莱克的《扫烟囱的孩子》(*The Chimney-Sweeper*)、《伦敦》(*London*)等诗作就准确而形象地刻画出了时代变迁所带来的英国社会的种种弊端以及底层普通老百姓艰难的生存状态。当然，同样以伦敦为背景，同样是表达对时局的担忧与不满，华兹华斯的笔法又有所不同。他采取了借古讽今的做法，通过呼唤弥尔顿这位英国历史上伟大改革家的名字，进而达到控诉伦敦城死气沉沉、毫无生机和活力的目的，表达出诗人渴望自由和民主的强烈呼声。

进入19世纪和20世纪，城市化进程在世界上各个地方已蔚为大观，成为一种不可逆转的趋势。一些欧美的大城市，诸如伦敦、巴黎、纽约等更成为城市发展的典范。在这样的背景之下，城市的文学艺术愈发呈现出蓬勃发展的态势。以美国为例，它的一些中心城市逐渐集聚起了一批拥有不同背景、来自不同阶层的小说家、画家、诗人和音乐家等，他们生活在城市的各个角落，呼吸着城市的气息，感受到了城市的脉动，自然而然地，他们也把创作的目光瞄准了城市生活的每一个细节。比如，在《草叶集》中，惠特曼就写下了多首以城市为题材的作品（包括 *To the States*、*On Journeys through the States*、*Starting from Paumanok*、*A Promise to California* 和 *City of Ships* 等）。这位19世纪美国最伟大的诗人之一，似乎天生就是美国梦的最佳代言人。他乐观开朗自信，在他的笔下，城市伟岸、雄健，犹如野草一般繁茂地成长，成为一个时代的记号。桑德堡是惠特曼之后另一位极具美国特色的大诗人，他的诗风豪迈、有力，充满刚性。桑德堡的《芝加哥诗抄》(*Chicago Poems*)名满诗坛，诗集中的 *Chicago*、*The Harbor*、*They Will Say*、

Skyscraper 和 *Chickens* 等从不同角度表现了城市生活以及诗人对新兴城市的思考。进入 20 世纪中期,在欧美各国、特别是美国,随着女性主义、反战以及反对种族歧视等政治思潮和文化运动的蓬勃开展,诗歌的作用和地位也在发生明显的变化。诗歌和城市、和生活在城市里的人们的呼声更加紧密地联系在了一起。"嚎叫派"诗人金斯堡等和旧金山文艺复兴之间的关系即是一个例证。

  城市,是诗歌诞生的地方。城市孕育了诗歌,诗歌反过来又推动了城市文化的发展。关于城市的诗歌,数不胜数,我们为大家所选取的这四首,只能说是沧海一粟,希望对于解读诗歌与城市之间的关系有所助益。

名篇导读

1. London①

William Blake

I wander thro'② each charter'd③ street,
Near where the charter'd Thames does flow.
And mark in every face I meet
Marks of weakness, marks of woe.

In every cry of every Man,
In every Infant's cry of fear,
In every voice, in every ban,
The mind-forg'd manacles I hear.

How the Chimney-sweeper's cry

Every black'ning④ Church appalls;

And the hapless⑤ Soldier's sigh

Runs in blood down Palace walls.

But most thro'midnight streets I hear

How the youthful Harlot's curse

Blasts the new born Infant's tear,

And blights with plagues the Marriage hearse.

【注释】

① 此诗选自英国诗人威廉·布莱克(William Blake,1757—1827)1794 年出版的诗集《经验之歌》(*Songs of Experience*)。

② thro':相当于 through。

③ charter'd:相当于 chartered。charter 原为动词,意为"特许",这里可理解为"特经……批准使用的"。第二小节第四行中的 mind-forg'd 相当于 mind-forged。

④ black'ning:相当于 blackening,这里作形容词,意为"黑暗的",修饰"Church"。

⑤ hapless:意为"不幸的,倒霉的"。

【作品赏析】

《伦敦》发表于 1794 年,时值法国大革命进行得如火如荼之际,而英国却与神圣罗马帝国、普鲁士、荷兰和西班牙等组成反法联盟,公然反对以"自由、平等、博爱"为口号的民主革命。在这样的背景下,作为英国政治经济中心的伦敦自然处在一片沉闷和压

第五章
诗歌与城市

抑的气氛之中。该诗即是诗人对当时英国当局实行的专制和暴政所发出的无声抗议,反映了诗人对英国下层阶级人民一贯的同情和对自由和民主的向往。

全诗虽仅有短短的十六行,却将伦敦这座城市的物、人以及笼罩在城市上空挥之不去的阴霾刻画得淋漓尽致。城市中的物,并不是纯粹地自然存在着,而是被统治者所占为己有。街道与河流也仿佛被刻上了统治者的印章,必须经过他们的特许批准才能够使用。生活在城市中的人们,特别是那些处在社会底层的普通百姓,更成为专制体制的牺牲品。他们的每一张面孔上都写满疲惫、虚弱与悲苦。在严苛的禁令之下,在人们痛苦的呻吟中,不谙世事的孩童惊恐不安的哭喊声所反映出来的,不仅仅是对人们身体的钳制,更是对心灵的禁锢。这是诗人眼中的大众在如此沉闷的城市中的生活状态。具体而言,诗人又进一步刻画出几类人群的生活状态:扫烟囱的孩子、不幸的士兵以及妓女和她的婴孩。在布莱克的诗中,扫烟囱的孩子是一个被经常提及的形象,他们身材瘦削、形容枯槁,小小年纪却被迫出卖苦力,在一个个狭长的烟囱里(包括那些宣扬仁爱的教堂的烟囱里)钻上爬下,过早地经受生活的磨难,有些人甚至因此而丢掉性命。无辜的士兵本不想参加战争,却被强制拖上了战场,他们无可奈何的叹息仿佛殷红的鲜血,滴洒在统治当局的围墙之外。当然,给诗人印象最深的还是深夜里听到的、年轻妓女对自己婴儿的大声诅咒。母亲对于自己的婴儿,本该显示出人性中最伟大的爱与包容,但在生活的压力下,母性被扭曲了,母亲对婴儿非但没有丝毫的爱,反而对婴儿发出了诅咒。这诅咒虽暂时止住了婴儿的啼哭,同时,却也宣告婚姻成为死亡的灵柩。在这里,年轻的妓女以一个思想上被褫夺的形象出现,她在夜里大声地诅咒本不应该出生的婴儿,又身不由己地将病菌传播出去,也将诅咒传播到其他的家庭之中。仿佛不仅仅在街道上处处可见处于悲惨境地的人们,在无数的家庭里,都存在着被诅咒过的人们。他们为这座城市劳作,却不幸遭到这座城市的唾弃。

  从写作技巧上来说,全诗共分为四小节,每节以 abab 押韵,形式颇为规整。此外,"重复"构成了该诗的一个很大的特点。例如,在第一节的前两行,诗人连续两次使用了 charter'd 一词,以突出伦敦(以及整个英国)自由的缺失以及专制铁幕的无处不在,表达出诗人对统治当局的不满。此外,在第一节最后以及第二节的开头三行,诗人又运用了重复的手段。在"Marks of weakness, marks of woe"和"In every cry of every Man, /In every Infant's cry of fear, /In every voice, in every ban"等几行中,诗人的语气沉重而坚决,犹如竭力控制自己情绪下发出的强力呐喊。在描绘出普通民众悲惨境遇的同时,诗人也表达出了自己的立场,即对生活在底层人们的同情和对当局者黑暗统治的不满和愤慨。

2. London[①]

Frank Stuart Flint

LONDON, my beautiful,
it is not the sunset
nor the pale green sky
shimmering through the curtain
of the silver birch[②],

nor the quietness;

it is not the hopping③

of birds

upon the lawn,

nor the darkness

stealing over all things

that moves me.

But as the moon creeps④ slowly

over the tree-tops

among the stars,

I think of her

and the glow her passing

sheds on men.

London, my beautiful,

I will climb

into the branches

to the moonlit⑤ tree-tops,

that my blood may be cooled

by the wind.

【诗人简介】弗兰克·斯图尔特·弗林特(Frank Stuart Flint, 1885—1960),20世纪英国意象派诗人,1913年在《诗刊》上发表《意象主义》一文,正式提出意象派的三条主要原则。

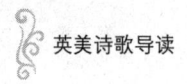

【注释】

① 本诗选自英国诗人弗林特于1915年出版的诗歌集《抑扬顿挫集》(*Cadences*)。

② birch：桦树；桦木。

③ hop：跳跃。

④ creep：爬行，慢慢地移动。

⑤ moonlit：被月光照亮的。

【作品赏析】

弗兰克·斯图尔特·弗林特是20世纪上半叶英国重要的诗人，曾被福特·马多克斯·福特誉为"这个国家最了不起和最优秀的灵魂之一"。弗林特主要以意象派得名，早年与休姆(T. E. Hulme)和庞德(Ezra Pound)等来往密切，为意象派诗歌的诞生和发展贡献良多。

在这首名为《伦敦》的作品中，弗林特着眼于"大伦敦"城中的"小事物"，通过对城市中傍晚时分的美景进行细致的梳理和描绘，对夕阳、蓝天、桦树、草坪、月色、繁星等意象的巧妙组合，突出了这座美丽的城市给诗人带来的情感上的冲击，同时也赋予了伦敦一种幽静的美。伦敦，这座城市一天的结束是从晚霞到来的时刻开始的：傍晚时分，透过斑驳的桦树颤抖的枝条，浅绿色的天空如水波般微微荡漾，这小小的"动"更加反衬出了整个傍晚的宁谧与安详。草坪光滑如织，小鸟时来啄食。这时，夜晚像一个不速之客，悄然来临，不露声色地将这一切美景全部装进口袋，悄悄带走。此情此景，仅仅在感官上，已经足够给人感动。可是，这还不够：月亮像一个智慧的老者，缓慢地，却又不着痕迹地升起。于是，上有众星围绕其间，下有翠树沐浴在皎洁的月光之下。此时的诗人，已不能不被感动了。这就是诗人眼中的伦敦，英伦三岛上的一颗明珠。这座城市一如夜空中的皓月,用她的光辉,恩泽着大地上的每一个人。在这样的景色之下,诗人的思绪被带到了很远的地方,想是那些前尘往事定会随着这思绪汹涌而出,不然,诗人为何竟要如贪玩的少年一般,爬到月光下的树上,好让习习的微风拂面而过,吹去血管中激荡的热情呢?

  同样是伦敦,这座20世纪的都会城市在诗人的笔下,既没有布莱克笔下令人不安的呻吟和号哭,也见不到现代化气息下一些大城市所凸显的呆板僵硬的一面。反其道而行之,诗人选择的视角却是极具"田园风范"的。诗人仿佛奔跑在树林中的孩童,陶醉在忘我的嬉戏和追逐之中。全诗呈现的是在傍晚和夜幕降临这样一个时刻,没有喧嚣,远离人群,人在城市中安歇,城市给人以惬意和享受。城市俨然成为一种"人化自然",成为了自然的一部分。从另一个角度来看,这何尝不是一种人与自然的融合。或许正是因为诗人心中有自然、有美、有爱,才能在纷扰的城市中准确地捕捉到一份宁谧的美,又或许,这也恰好体现出诗人"大隐隐于市"的达观与对人生和世事的坦然。

  这首诗用词简单,意象清晰、鲜明、灵动:黄昏、落日、浅绿色的天空、桦树、鸟、草坪、夜幕、月亮、繁星一一跃然眼前。此外,全诗虽没有统一的押韵,但阅读起来连贯流畅,给人以清新自然的感觉,不愧为意象派的名作。

3. City of Orgies[①]

Walt Whitman

  CITY of orgies, walks and joys,

City whom that I have lived and sung in your midst will one day make you illustrious,

Not the pageants② of you, not your shifting tableaus③, your spectacles, repay me,

Not the interminable④ rows of your houses, nor the ships at the wharves,

Nor the processions in the streets, nor the bright windows with goods in them,

Nor to converse with learn'd persons, or bear my share in the soiree⑤ or feast;

Not those, but as I pass O Manhattan, your frequent and swift flash of eyes offering me love,

Offering response to my own — these repay me,

Lovers, continual lovers, only repay me.

【诗人简介】沃尔特·惠特曼(Walt Whitman, 1819—1892),美国诗人,人文主义者。作者在诗歌形式上有大胆创新,创造了"自由体"的诗歌形式,节奏自由奔放。代表作有诗集《草叶集》。

【注释】

① 此诗选自美国著名诗人沃尔特·惠特曼于1855年出版的诗集《草叶集》(*Leaves of Grass*)。标题中的 orgies 为 orgy 的复数形式,意为"狂欢"。

② pageant:盛会,露天表演。

③ tableaus:生动的场面。

④ interminable:冗长的,无休止的。

⑤ soiree：晚会，社交聚会。

【作品赏析】

　　对于城市，人们往往会形成与乡村截然不同的印象：乡村是悠闲的、接近自然的、宁静而安详的；而城市给人的最初印象则莫过于充斥着喧哗与骚动。在很多人看来，大城市的繁华、忙碌和斑驳陆离固然代表着城市的魅力和气魄，但与此同时，也的确常常使很多身处其中的人生出远离嘈杂和纷扰、渴望回归自然的想法。但是，作为土生土长的纽约人，惠特曼却不这样认为。在他看来，城市，就像他诗中的乡村一样，也处处充满着一种独特的气息，这种气息无时无刻不在吸引着人们热爱城市，热爱城市中的生活。《狂欢的城市》一诗即刻画出了诗人对城市生活的由衷赞美。

　　该诗用了大部分的篇幅描写城市生活的场景：一座处在狂欢中的城市，脚步纷杂、熙来攘往的人流，宾朋满座的盛会，精彩的演出和人头攒动的场面，一排排齐整的街区，码头上依次停靠的轮船，街道上车水马龙，商店的橱窗里各色商品琳琅满目，彬彬有礼的人们穿梭其间、谈笑风生……在这些生动的城市即景之中，诗人或许仅是作为一个旁观者在观察，未必亲身体验其中。反过来说，设想他是一位成功人士，拥有这个城市的所有繁荣和奢靡，他却也未必能真正感到心灵的满足。诗人写道，当"我"处于人海中，接触到擦肩而过的人投来的温热的目光，"我"顿时感受到了爱的力量。原来，诗人所看重的并非城市的躯壳，它那高高耸立的大楼、宽阔的街道、热闹的商店，以及城市所代表的无穷财富，相反，他所赞赏的是城市的内涵，也就是它的气质和灵魂。在诗人看来，曼哈顿固然是极尽繁华之地，但是，更可宝贵的是这里的人们相互之间保有着一份关爱和真情，这才是这座城市赠与他的最好礼物。所谓芸芸众生皆是爱人，在惠特曼笔下，这也是现代大都市所应有的品格。

惠特曼不愧为划时代的诗坛巨匠，他的这首《狂欢的城市》在今天这个商品经济高度发达的时代尤其显出它的独特之处。他在诗中倡导的和谐与爱正是我们所亟须的，他为我们奉上的是一场心灵的狂欢；或者也可以说，他以诗人的胆识预言了未来城市发展的方向。

从创作手法来看，这是一首典型的惠特曼式的作品。全诗不押韵，诗行长短不一，展现出奔放自由、简洁流畅的特点。诗人以通俗的语言入诗，通过对"not"的多次重复，一方面表现城市生活的变幻多姿，另一方面也起到了强调的作用。此外，"S"音贯穿全诗，使得全诗读起来有一种紧凑感和独特的节奏感，仿佛在引导读者跟着诗人的脚步行走在曼哈顿的街道上。

4. Chicago[①]

Carl Sandburg

HOG[②] Butcher for the World,
　　Tool Maker, Stacker[③] of Wheat,
　　Player with Railroads[④] and the Nation's Freight Handler;
　　Stormy, husky[⑤], brawling[⑥],
　　City of the Big Shoulders[⑦]:

They tell me you are wicked and I believe them, for I have seen your painted women⑧ under the gas lamps luring the farm boys.

And they tell me you are crooked⑨ and I answer: Yes, it is true I have seen the gunman kill and go free to kill again.

And they tell me you are brutal and my reply is: On the faces of women and children I have seen the marks of wanton⑩ hunger.

And having answered so I turn once more to those who sneer at this my city, and I give them back the sneer and say to them:

Come and show me another city with lifted head singing so proud to be alive and coarse and strong and cunning.

Flinging magnetic curses⑪ amid the toil of piling job on job, here is a tall bold slugger⑫ set vivid against the little soft cities;

Fierce as a dog with tongue lapping for action, cunning as a savage pitted against

the wilderness,

Bareheaded,

Shoveling,

Wrecking,

Planning,

Building, breaking, rebuilding,

Under the smoke, dust all over his mouth, laughing with white teeth,

Under the terrible burden of destiny laughing as a young man laughs,
Laughing even as an ignorant fighter laughs who has never lost a battle,
Bragging⑬ and laughing that under his wrist is the pulse, and under his ribs the heart of the people,
　　　　Laughing!
Laughing the stormy, husky, brawling laughter of Youth, half-naked, sweating, proud to be Hog Butcher, Tool Maker, Stacker of Wheat, Player with Railroads and Freight Handler to the Nation.

【诗人简介】卡尔·桑德堡(Carl Sandburg, 1878—1967), 美国诗人、传记作家和编辑, 善于以通俗的语言入诗, 作品多以芝加哥为背景, 反映美国工业化扩张以及中西部的风土人情和人文精神, 被誉为"人民的诗人"。作品曾三获普利策奖。

【注释】
① 此诗选自美国诗人桑德堡于1916年出版的诗集《芝加哥诗抄》(*Chicago Poems*)。
② hog: 生猪或野猪。
③ stacker: 货栈或堆场所使用的堆包机。
④ Player with Railroads: 指芝加哥是美国的铁路运输枢纽。
⑤ husky: 孔武有力的, 刚猛的。
⑥ brawling: 咆哮的; 怒吼的。
⑦ City of the Big Shoulders: 桑德堡把芝加哥称之为"肩膀

宽阔的城市",该称谓现已成为芝加哥的别称之一。

⑧ painted women:这里指涂脂抹粉、浓妆艳服的妓女。

⑨ crooked:没有操守的,不择手段的。

⑩ wanton:肆无忌惮的,赤裸裸的。

⑪ flinging magnetic curses:fling 的基本意思是"抛出或扔出",这里是一种夸张的用法,表示"大声喊出"。所谓 magnetic curses,也属于夸张的用法,意思是"带有磁性的诅咒"。

⑫ slugger:原指棒球比赛中的强力击球手,或拳击比赛中出拳很重的拳手,这里是一种比喻,喻指芝加哥是一个充满活力的城市。

⑬ bragging:吹牛,胡侃。

【作品赏析】

卡尔·桑德堡是美国芝加哥文艺复兴浪潮中的核心人物,他的诗歌以歌颂城市、歌颂工业文明而出名。1916 年的《芝加哥诗抄》(*Chicago Poems*)、1918 年的《剥玉米的人》(*Cornhuskers*)和 1920 年的《烟与钢》(*Smoke and Steel*)是这方面的代表作。《芝加哥》一诗最初是以"芝加哥"命名的 9 首诗歌中的第一首,1914 年首次刊印在门罗主编的《诗刊》上,后被收录进诗人的第一部诗集《芝加哥诗抄》。这首诗是在美国社会工业化和城市化扩张的大背景下写就的,机械化大生产、拔地而起的高楼大厦、如火如荼的西进运动、铁路网络的不断延伸等,一切都处在急剧的变化之中。这首诗也是一个城市人对着他的城市唱出的雄浑、壮阔的赞歌,它激越、高亢、嘹亮,充满着野性的力量和原始的本真。桑德堡出生在伊利诺伊,1912 年他来到了这座州内最大(在全美国也是数一数二)的城市,随即被它的"暴躁、魁梧和喧闹"所吸引,于是写下了这首赞美芝加哥强悍、粗犷、狂浪不拘性格的传世之作。

诗歌开篇,桑德堡把芝加哥描绘成是一个世界工业和贸易的中心,这里有世界上最大的屠宰场,有各种各样工具的制造厂商,高高的小麦仓库,纵横交错的铁路线,有全美国货物运输的中转基地,等等。他用了一连串不同寻常的比喻,短促有力、令人印象深刻,特别是第四行三个并列的形容词 stormy, husky, brawling,更是一语中的,点出了芝加哥独具特色的雄性气质和魅力。在随后的几行,诗人以接连的平行结构长句,通过"They tell me you are … and I answer(他们告诉我,你……,而我却要说……)"这样的句式,全方位地展示了一个更加真实的西部大都市形象。他并没有回避芝加哥的灰暗和不幸,这座城市里,也有不尽如人意的事情发生。浓妆艳抹的妓女在昏黄的路灯下勾引少不更事的农场小伙,冷血枪手杀人事件时有发生,儿童和妇人的脸上写着饥饿,等等。但是,诗人随即笔锋一转,若是有人想要借题发挥,因而对这座城市加以蔑视和嘲笑,他却要坚决地予以还击。在他眼里,还有哪一座城市能如此高昂起头颅大声地、骄傲地歌唱,歌声中充满活泼、粗犷、强壮与机敏?还有哪一座城市能够如此简单、快乐,即便在堆积如山的工作面前也只是抛出几句带有磁性的诅咒而已?惟有芝加哥,他是城市中的另类,犹如一个高大英武的拳击手,又像一条时刻准备战斗的猎犬,或者像茫茫荒野里的野蛮人。他光着头,挥着锹,毁灭、计划、建设、破坏、再建设,肆意而为。请注意,此处连续出现的7个定义芝加哥的单词,和前面的长句构成了极大的反差。接着,诗人又延续了此前对芝加哥的赞美,仍然是平行结构的长句,仍然是拟人化的手法,现在的芝加哥已化身成了一个年轻的小伙子,在烟雾和灰尘缭绕之中,在命运的重压下,他一如既往、肆无忌惮地放声大笑。他像一个从未在战场失利的无知无畏的士兵,自负、骄傲、开心地笑着。他放浪形骸、狂笑不止,在震天的笑声中建立起了世界上最大的屠宰场,各种各样工具的制造厂商,高高的小麦仓库,纵横交错的铁路线和全美国货物运输的中转基地。诗歌末尾,桑德堡重复了开篇建构的意象,使芝加哥的城市形象进一步固化。

总的来说,这是一首美国式的城市交响曲,通篇气势磅礴,又张弛有度,读起来一气呵成。诗人从头至尾采用拟人化的手法,将芝加哥比喻为一个粗犷、骄傲、活力无穷的劳动者,可以说,将拟人化的手法运用到了极致。此外,该诗的语言也极具特色:随意、不加修饰和生活化,与诗歌所要表现的城市粗犷的形象相得益彰。它和惠特曼的诗歌一样,有一种浑然而成的力量弥散其间。

小 结

诗歌与城市,或者说,城市与诗歌,它们之间总有着说不完的故事。从某种意义上来说,凡是诗歌,无不与城市存在着这样或那样的联系。即便是歌咏田园乡村的诗歌,也往往不过是取了与城市相对立的角度来观察而已,它仍然离不开"城市"这个参照物。

作为城市文明的一个有机组成部分,诗歌对于城市的重要性是不言而喻的。首先,诗歌可以成为城市文明的歌颂者和传播者。城市是摩登的代名词,城市里有便捷的交通、宽阔的街道,有高楼大厦和令人眼花缭乱的霓虹灯,还有画廊、博物馆和电影院。城市的一切美好需要有人去发现和描摹,这样才能点燃起光荣和梦想的火把,激励城市内外的人们继续不断追求、不断超越。发表于20世纪初期的《芝加哥》可以说是一部赞美芝加哥城市形象的英雄史诗。诗歌中的芝加哥高大、强健、有力,那里到处都是热火朝天的生产场面,那里的人们乐观、开朗,充满自信。尽管它远非十全十美，尽管也会看到贫困、犯罪和欺诈，但是，作为美国中西部的第一大都市，桑德堡笔下的芝加哥绝对是一个正面、阳光和朝气蓬勃的所在。可以想象，多少年来，这首《芝加哥》必定曾经激励了无数年轻人投向它热情的怀抱。弗林特的《伦敦》有点特别，它更像是一支赞美城市的小夜曲。这首诗中固然没有出现泰晤士河，没有伦敦塔的影子，也不见白金汉宫、大英博物馆或莎士比亚剧院等。但是，诗人不愧是一个善于捕捉细节的意象派大师，他抓住了伦敦城繁华喧嚣背后安静宁谧的那一刻，通过月夜、星星、树梢和小鸟等意象的精巧叠加，向读者展示了伦敦城的另一种美。这首诗充满了一位诗人对一座城市的真挚热爱，感情细腻而又深沉，读来又有一份不一样的感动。

不过，诗歌有时候也充当着城市批判者的角色。城市，往往代表着国家的心脏，是政治、经济和文化特权的集中之地，对城市阴暗面的曝光和批判实质就意味着对国家和体制的不满和抗议。威廉·布莱克的《伦敦》就是一个典型的例子。时值工业革命和机器化大生产的背景之下，布莱克笔下的伦敦却是一个哀鸿遍地、贫病交加的死亡之地。作为工业革命的发源地，伦敦城虽然因此而得益并获得了迅速的发展，但与此同时也带来了诸多的问题。城市中因传统手工业衰落而引发的失业现象十分严重，贫富差距不断扩大，居于社会底层的百姓普遍不堪生活的重负，境遇极为悲惨。而另一方面，当时的政治气候却十分紧张，当局者采取高压政策，不仅对民生疾苦不闻不问，甚至还竭力压制民众的呼声。于是，布莱克的《伦敦》就在这样的环境下出现了，它是为这个城市而写的一曲挽歌，更是对政府当局发出的义正词严的控诉状。诗人是一个特殊的群体，他们观察敏锐、感情细腻，更加难能可贵的是，在很多情况下，他们还能勇敢地承担起社会良心的责任。

第五章
诗歌与城市

当然,城市的灵魂是生活在里面的人,是他们的生存状态、言行举止,他们的精神风貌以及他们的追求和失落。城市之所以发展、壮大并成为人们趋之若鹜的理想之地,不仅在于它的繁华和物质上的享受,更重要的还在于它的气质和内涵;而一个城市的底蕴却绝非一朝一夕就能建立起来,它需要几代人、甚至几十代人长期共同的努力才能达成。正如惠特曼在《狂欢的城市》里所描写的,城市的街道、商店和热闹的聚会等虽然令人迷恋,但真正令人陶醉并为之骄傲的还是人们眼睛里放射出的爱的光华。爱,有无穷的力量,它也是推动城市和整个社会前进的原动力。不过,城市生活也是多层次和多侧面的,既有阳光和爱的温暖,就必定也会遇到风雨和坎坷。比如,我们在"扩展阅读篇目"一栏里列出的兰斯顿·休斯的《疲惫的布鲁斯》(*The Weary Blues*)和埃德温·鲁宾逊的《理查德·科利》(*Richard Cory*)这两首诗描写的就是城市人的另一种生活。前者讲的是纽约黑人惨淡的人生,作品中的主人公一无所有,唯有疲惫的布鲁斯相伴;而后者则是物质富有、灵魂虚无的城市白人,虽然表面上看事业成功、受人尊敬,但内心却极度空虚,最终只能以自杀来寻求解脱。

扩展阅读篇目

A London Summer Morning by Mary Robinson
London 1802 by William Wordsworth
Composed upon Westminster Bridge by William Wordsworth
A Tale of Two Cities by Rudyard Kipling
Sonnet on Approaching Italy by Oscar Wilde
Richard Cory by Edwin Arlington Robinson
To You by Walt Whitman

The Weary Blues by Langston Hughes
Sonnet: O City, City by Delmore Schwartz
To Brooklyn Bridge by Hart Crane
Patterson by William Carlos Williams
Window by Carl Sandberg
The City Limits by A. R. Ammons
Young in New Orleans by Charles Bukowski

第六章

诗歌与田园

点 题

A lake is the landscape's most beautiful and expressive feature. It is earth's eye; looking into which the beholder measures the depth of his own nature.

—— From *Walden* by Henry David Thoreau

诗歌是一个包罗万象的大花园,而山水田园诗则是这座花园中不可或缺的一块花圃。中国的山水田园诗源远流长,在最早的诗歌集《诗经》里,就有描写山水田园的清新诗句:"七月在野,八月在宇,九月在户,十月蟋蟀入我床下。"(《七月》)历经唐宋、魏晋,山水田园诗逐渐成为中国文学传统的一个重要方面。田园之美,世代同歌。"采菊东篱下,悠然见南山"(陶渊明《饮酒》)、"明月松间照,清泉石上流"(王维《山居秋暝》),此等脍炙人口的诗句经过时间的洗练,代代相传,吟唱出了东方人对自然的热爱和赞美。

在中国的文学传统中,素来就有"山川之美,古来共谈"(陶弘景《答谢中书书》)之说,而在英美诗歌的天地里,也处处回荡着歌咏山川湖泊之美的自然交响曲。从英格兰美丽的湖畔风光,到北美广袤深邃的土地,大自然以它博大雄奇的胸襟孕育出了一批又一批的杰出诗人。英美诗歌虽没有"田园诗"一说,但描写田园、山水的诗歌却绝不在少数。与中国的山水田园诗相比较,英美文学中表现山水田园风貌的诗歌一般呈现出以下几方面的特点:

首先,英美描写山水田园的诗歌不成派别。历代以来,无论英美,虽曾涌现出不少以描写自然风物见长的大诗人,比如英国的华兹华斯、济慈、丁尼生和美国的布莱恩特、惠特曼等,但往往仅以个体的形象活跃在诗坛,最多被冠以"具有自然情结的诗人"这样的头衔,却鲜有因对田园自然风光的共同爱好进而形成诗歌流派的情况出现。在英国,虽有"湖畔派"诗人这样以描写自然意趣为特色的诗人团体出现,但也只是个别现象。就英美诗歌总体而言,纯粹描写自然山水风光的诗歌所占的比例不具备数量上的优势。单就诗歌主题论,涉及人生、爱情、战争、死亡和国家前途等类型的诗歌还是占到多数。

其次,在描写对象上,英美描写山水田园的诗歌多擅长以小见大,其虽涉及山水花草、人鱼鸟兽等,但常常是一些微小的、单独的个体。这一点与中国的山水田园诗形成了很大的区别。中国山水田园诗既有描写单独的植物、花鸟的诗歌,也不乏描写蔚为壮观的名山大川的大气之作。这恐怕和诗人所处国家的地理环境也有一定的关系。中国自古以来就地大物博、山川壮阔,因此咏颂山水的诗句十分常见。而在英美,特别是英国,其地势低平,多以平原为主,故此描写壮阔河山的诗句相比之下也就少了。

再次,英美的山水田园主题诗歌中,纯粹描写自然之美的诗歌并不多见,其间或多或少都夹杂着诗人的思想和感情。而且,理性思考和哲学性的思辨又占了很大一个部分:或是对人生、或是对社会、或是对艺术的永恒和美本身的思考。这和欧美文化的思维方式有着千丝万缕的联系。欧洲历经16世纪的文艺复兴运动和

第六章
诗歌与田园

17、18世纪的启蒙运动,逐渐树立起对理性的追逐和信仰,理性哲学思潮尤为盛行。在这种思潮的影响下,理性思维成为西方占主流地位的思维方式。在文学艺术领域,理性的思维方式也潜移默化地影响着西方作家的创作。即使有华兹华斯的名句"诗歌是感情的自然流露",英美诗歌中仍处处可以看到渗透在感性之外的理性思维的影子。

最后,英美的田园诗和中国传统的山水田园诗之间还存在着一个很大的不同点,那就是英美的田园诗中相当一部分都包含有对生态的忧思。这和诗歌的发展、特别是社会的发展变化轨迹有着密不可分的联系。众所周知,英美诗歌在近代的迅速崛起,或称现代化之路始于19世纪之后,而这一时期,恰逢西方开始其工业化进程。工业化和城市化固然造就了西方的物质繁荣和人民生活富足,但与此同时也带来了一系列的环境问题。处在时代前列的诗人以其敏锐的洞察力,率先觉察到工业化进程所带来的负面影响,其中之一就是对环境的损害和破坏。因此反映生态危机、倡导保护生态、爱护自然的诗歌的出现也是一种必然。

需要加以指出的是,在英美文坛,虽然以自然和田园为主题的诗作在数量上不占优势,也未曾涌现蔚为大观的以"田园"得名的诗歌流派,但是,细细品味,仍不乏众多优秀之作。它们有的擅长饱含深情地描摹、歌颂自然之大美,有的因感叹于自然的种种而发出对宇宙、对人生和家国的深邃思考,又有的则在字里行间透出了对人与自然关系日益恶化和生态危机逼近的忧思。总之,英美的田园主题诗歌篇目众多,体系庞杂,仅少数几篇远远不能概括其全貌。然而,沧海拾珠,我们从以上所提及的几个方面作为切入点,从大量优秀的诗篇中选取四首来进行介绍和品赏,希望达到管窥一得的效果。

名篇导读

1. The World Is Too Much with Us①
William Wordsworth

The world is too much with us; late and soon,
Getting and spending, we lay waste our powers;
　Little we see in Nature that is ours;
We have given our hearts away, a sordid boon!②
　This Sea that bares her bosom to the moon;
　The winds that will be howling at all hours,
And are up-gathered now like sleeping flowers;
　For this, for everything, we are out of tune;
　It moves us not. — Great God! I'd rather be
　　A Pagan③ suckled in a creed outworn;
　So might I, standing on this pleasant lea④,
Have glimpses that would make me less forlorn⑤;
　Have sight of Proteus⑥ rising from the sea;
　Or hear old Triton⑦ blow his wreathed horn.

【诗人简介】威廉·华兹华斯(William Wordsworth, 1770—1850),英国浪漫主义诗人,湖畔诗人之一。代表作有与塞缪尔·泰勒·柯勒律治合著的《抒情歌谣集》,长诗《序曲》、《漫游》等。

【注释】

① 此诗由英国浪漫主义诗人威廉·华兹华斯作于 1802 年，后被收入于 1807 年出版的诗集《两卷诗》(Poems, In Two Volumes)。

② sordid boon：这是一个矛盾的说法：sordid 的意思是"污秽的"，而 boon 的意思是"恩惠"。诗人把这两个词放在一起，暗指工业文明和物质上的繁荣乃是一种让人既爱又恨的结果。

③ pagan：异教徒。

④ lea：诗歌用语，草地，草原。

⑤ forlorn：诗歌用语，忧伤的，悲伤的。

⑥ Proteus：早期希腊神话中的一个海神，以变幻莫测的相貌和拥有预知未来的能力而著称。

⑦ Triton：希腊神话中人身鱼尾的海神，据说常随身携带一个海螺壳，用来作为号角以激起海浪。

【作品赏析】

作为 19 世纪英国浪漫主义诗歌的杰出代表，华兹华斯擅长对自然景物的描写与刻画。他笔下的一草一木多清新秀丽，诗歌多节奏明快，字里行间洋溢着诗人对自然的热爱和赞美之情。他的一些名作，如《我好似一朵流云独自漫游》(I Wandered Lonely as a Cloud)、《黄昏散步》(An Evening Walk)、《致杜鹃》(To the Cuckoo)、《我心雀跃》(My Heart Leaps up) 和《威斯敏斯特桥上》(Composed upon Westminster Bridge) 等都从不同的角度勾画出了自然纯美的意境以及诗人陶醉其中的自得和惬意。不过，这首《我们太沉湎于俗世》却有所不同。这首诗歌中虽有对自然美景的描述之语，但其着眼点却在于揭示当时工业化背景下人们对环境

的漠视，表现出诗人对于人与自然和谐发展的长远目光。

英国自18世纪60年代即开始了工业革命的步伐。伴随着经济的发展，人们生活上的富足和物质上的享受也成为可能。在这种情况下，整个英国社会变得浮躁起来，人们追逐金钱，贪图享乐。与此同时，他们和周围原本亲密无间的山川鸟兽、一草一木却变得陌生了、疏离了。他们对自己身边的自然美景熟视无睹，甚至根本不懂得如何去珍惜和爱护。走在时代前列的诗人这时展现出了他们敏锐的洞察力，华兹华斯的这首诗歌就是一个很好的例子。该诗开头以恳切的言辞描绘出人与自然之间不和谐的关系：我们从这个世界不断地索取又不断地消耗，我们自私自利，丝毫不为自己的所作所为感到羞愧。月光下的海洋敞开胸怀似乎在拥抱安详的夜与周遭的世界，风不露一丝动静似乎在积蓄力量等待怒号……面对这样如画的风景，很多人既感受不到它的美，更不会为之动容，反而已经变得麻木和不以为然了。这样的情形使华兹华斯这位热爱自然的诗人忧心忡忡，一句"Great God"将全诗分为两个部分：此句之前是对人与自然不和谐关系的列举，字里行间充满着诗人对人类所作所为的隐忍的讽刺与对环境的惋惜，此句之后诗人并未道出"人类"这一群体该怎么做——仿佛是对人类已失望至极——而是面对自然、面对人类对自然的破坏，"我"慨然表示宁愿做一个异教徒，回到原始的、被遗弃的信仰里，回到希腊神话描述的自然纯美里。惟有如此，在面对自然的时候，"我"才不会感到那么孤单。这是一种他人无法理解的孤寂感，更是一种"众人皆醉我独醒"的无奈。

该诗采用意大利十四行诗的样式，以 abba abba cdcdcd 形式押韵，韵律优美，读起来朗朗上口。此外，在选词和用词上也可以看出诗人的匠心独运之处。开篇第一句中的 too much 一词直接有力,给人以先入为主的强烈印象,紧随其后的 late and soon 更加深了这种印象。"late"和"soon"表面上看似矛盾,却清楚地揭示了"我们"在这个世界上每时每刻所感受到的困乏和不能承受之重。第二行中的 getting and spending 又是两个相反意义单词的连用,将人类轻而易举地得到又不加珍惜地挥霍的形象表现得淋漓尽致。在全篇的最后两行,连续出现了两个希腊神话传说中的海神 Proteus 和 Triton,不但提升了作品的厚重感和历史感,也再次表明了诗人对于珍惜和爱护自然环境的态度。

2. The Skylark①

John Clare

The rolls and harrows② lie at rest beside
The battered road; and spreading far and wide
Above the russet③ clods④, the corn is seen
Sprouting its spiry points of tender green,
Where squats the hare, to terrors wide awake,
Like some brown clod the harrows failed to break.
Opening their golden caskets to the sun,
The buttercups⑤ make schoolboys eager run,
To see who shall be first to pluck the prize —
Up from their hurry, see, the skylark flies,
And o'er⑥ her half-formed nest, with happy wings
Winnows the air, till in the cloud she sings,
Then hangs a dust-spot in the sunny skies,

And drops, and drops, till in her nest she lies,

Which they unheeded passed — not dreaming then

That birds which flew so high would drop agen⑦

To nests upon the ground, which anything

May come at to destroy. Had they the wing

Like such a bird, themselves would be too proud,

And build on nothing but a passing cloud!

As free from danger as the heavens are free

From pain and toil, there would they build and be,

And sail about the world to scenes unheard

Of and unseen — Oh, were they but a bird!

So think they, while they listen to its song,

And smile and fancy and so pass along;

While its low nest, moist with the dews of morn,

Lies safely, with the leveret⑧, in the corn.

【诗人简介】 约翰·克莱尔(John Clare, 1793—1864), 英国诗人, 出身农民。他的诗主要写自然景色与农村风光。诗集有《村子里的歌手》(1821)、《牧人日历》(1827)、《乡村缪斯》(1835)。

【注释】

① 此诗选自英国诗人约翰·克莱尔于1835年出版的诗集《乡村缪斯》(*The Rural Muse*)。

② rolls and harrows: 农民耕作时用的犁耙。

③ russet: 赤褐色, 黄褐色。

④ clod: 土块。

⑤ buttercup：毛茛属植物。
⑥ o'er：相当于 over。
⑦ agen：相当于 again，再次。
⑧ leveret：小野兔。

【作品赏析】

　　约翰·克莱尔素有英国"农民诗人"和"乡土诗人"之誉，其诗歌以对自然景物和乡村风貌的生动描述而著称。20 世纪后期，随着生态文学的兴起，克莱尔及其作品已越来越引起读者和评论界的关注。这首《云雀》选自诗人最后一部、也是其最受赞誉的诗集《乡村缪斯》。

　　乡村的农忙时节还未到来，闲置的农具被堆放在路边。由于久置不用，农具的颜色和泥土的土黄色浑然一体。路边的野兔警觉地竖起耳朵，像是随时防备未知的敌人和危险。旁边的玉米地里，玉米在抽穗。孩子们已经放学，看着前面阳光下盛开的金色花朵，他们欢快地奔跑，想要比试谁能第一个摘到那些花朵。这突如其来的动作惊扰了云雀，云雀离巢而飞，穿过云端，唱起歌来。它们越飞越高，晴朗的天空下，变成了黑色的小点，继而又徐徐落下，回到了鸟巢。孩子们径自追跑，对这一切浑然不觉。他们或许想不到，飞得这么高的云雀，最终也会落在地上的鸟巢里，而鸟巢也随时有可能被毁坏。孩子们听着云雀的歌，流露出无限的羡慕和遐想。假设这些孩子们有着云雀一样的翅膀，他们定会因为可以直达云端而感到无比自豪。流云之上，犹如天堂，自由而没有隐忧。那时，他们就可以周游世界，看前所未见，听前所未闻。带着这些幻想，孩子们微笑着跑过。云雀的鸟巢沾着清晨湿漉漉的水珠，在玉米地里安然无恙。

　　这是一幅由三个场景交错并置构成的乡村图：第一个场景是

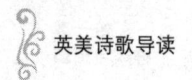

闲置的农具静静地躺在路边,看似随意,却勾画出了整个背景的闲适和静谧。第二个场景是一群放学而归的孩子,他们的"跑"一方面和农具的"静"构成对比,另一方面也为云雀的"飞"做了铺垫。同时,一群孩子为了第一个摘到花而你追我赶的场景,更表现出了孩子们的天真烂漫,这也为诗的后半部分,即孩子们自由的想象做了铺垫。第三个场景是云雀的起飞和降落。该诗难能可贵的地方是,诗人不仅仅简单地描述了这三个场景,而是由云雀的起飞引发联想,由云雀的"飞之高"又"降之低",由孩子们看到云雀飞得高而心生羡慕到这表面的光鲜背后不为人知的潜在的危险而引发出一系列思考。这也就间接地点出了该诗的主题,即在于反映出生命的脆弱和不确定性。值得注意的是,诗人通篇并没有发出正面的提问,也没有作任何主观的评价,相反,他通过巧妙的安排引导读者置身其中,并启发读者进行深入的思考。

  从创作技巧层面上看,该诗每两句一个韵脚,诵读起来朗朗上口。在用词方面,成对词语的运用,诸如 rolls and harrows, far and wide, pain and toil,取得了节奏上明快的效果,加强了诗歌的韵律美。另外,最后两句"While its low nest, moist with the dews of morn,/Lies safely, with the leveret, in the corn."仿佛云雀又回到了未被惊扰而起飞的状态,前后构成一种呼应的效果,也给全诗留下无穷的回味。

3. Stopping by Woods on a Snowy Evening①
Robert Frost

Whose woods these are I think I know.

His house is in the village though;
He will not see me stopping here
To watch his woods fill up with snow.

My little horse must think it queer
To stop without a farmhouse near
Between the woods and frozen lake.
The darkest evening of the year.

He gives his harness bells a shake②
To ask if there is some mistake.
The only other sound's the sweep
Of easy wind and downy flake③.

The woods are lovely, dark and deep,
But I have promises to keep,
And miles to go before I sleep,
And miles to go before I sleep.

【诗人简介】罗伯特·弗罗斯特(Robert Frost, 1874—1963),美国诗人,曾四度获得普利策奖。主要创作抒情短诗和叙事诗,诗歌风格质朴清新、涵义隽永,寓深刻的哲理思考于简洁朴实的诗句中。

【注释】
① 此诗选自美国诗人罗伯特·弗罗斯特于1923年出版的诗

集《新罕布什尔》(*New Hampshire*)。

② He gives his harness bells a shake：意为"马儿轻轻地摇了摇马具上的铃铛"。

③ downy flake：柔细的雪片。

【作品赏析】

　　罗伯特·弗罗斯特是美国20世纪最受欢迎的诗人之一,曾四次获得普利策诗歌奖。弗罗斯特的诗歌以语言通俗、简明、富于哲理而著称,其作品多在描写生活中普通场景之际点出不为他人所悟出的哲思。比如,一般读者比较熟悉的《未选择的路》(*The Road Not Taken*),黄色的树林里,两条路出现在眼前,诗人选择了人迹罕至的一条。通过对于路的选择,诗人暗示了自己对于人生之路的抉择。同样,这一首《雪夜林边小驻》则以一个雪夜林间短暂的停留作为出发点,抒发了诗人对人生和责任的思考。

　　在一个冬日傍晚,诗人牵着马在一处树林边停留了片刻。幽静如处子般的自然给了诗人无限的灵感和思考。如果诗歌是有颜色的,这首诗则是白色的,白色的雪覆盖住了近处的树林和远处结满冰的湖面;如果诗歌是流动的,这首诗则是相对静止的;如果诗歌是有声音的,这首诗则是安静的。行人绝迹,一人一马站立在林前,没有对话没有喧嚣。马具上的铃铛声、轻风、落雪的声音反而使得周围的环境显得愈加宁谧。在冬日的傍晚遇见这样一处风景也许只是偶然,但是,显然这不是诗人第一次路过此地,诗人一开始就已指出:"Whose woods these are I think I know."既然诗人认识这树林的主人,想必在此之前一定知道它的存在。平日的树林可能没有什么特殊之处,但正是这么一个宁谧的夜晚触动了诗人的心境。林子很美,幽深黑暗,如果能在此停留、歇息亦未尝不是一件好事。但是,在诗歌的结尾处,诗人笔锋一转——But I have promises to keep, /And miles to go before I sleep, /And miles to go before I sleep. 出乎读者的意料,成为全诗的点睛之笔,将该诗提升为诗人对生活、对人生的品味和反思。前面看似简单的风景描写,特别是 frozen lake, the darkest evening of the year 等似乎是诗人不留痕迹埋下的伏笔,也许预示着生活的不尽如人意之处。此情此景,是选择停下劳累的步伐在此歇息还是继续前行?诗人给出的答案是,他无意在此久留,他选择了在休息之前继续前行。这似乎在暗示,虽然人生之路上不时会有艰险,也难免会感到倦怠,但承诺和责任高于一切。在最终的目的地没有到达、承诺未曾兑现之前,他必须克服困难继续前行。诗歌结尾处的重复"And miles to go before I sleep."一咏三叹,一方面反衬出景色的诱人令诗人难以割舍,另一方面更加突出了诗人继续前行的决心。

这首诗共分为四个小节,每小节一、三、四句押韵,节奏感较强。特别是全诗从头至尾都有一个"s"音贯穿其中,在听觉上增加了一种韵律的统一,视觉上又将全诗连贯为一体。弗罗斯特的诗歌特点之一就是用词简洁、凝练,善于把生活化的语汇融入诗歌,本诗亦不例外。

4. ALBA[①]

William Stanley Merwin

Climbing in the mist I came to a terrace wall[②]
and saw above it a small field of broad beans in flower

their white fragrance was flowing through the first light
of morning there a little way up the mountain
where I had made my way through the olive groves
and under the blossoming boughs of the almonds③
above the old hut of the charcoal burner
where suddenly the scent of the bean flowers found me
and as I took the next step I heard
the creak of the harness and the mule's shod hooves
striking stones in the furrow and then the low voice
of the man talking softly praising the mule
as he walked behind through the cloud in his white shirt
along the row and between his own words
he was singing under his breath a few phrases
at a time of the same song singing it
to his mule it seemed as I listened
watching their breaths and not understanding a word

【诗人简介】威廉·斯坦利·默温(William Stanley Merwin, 1927—),美国最著名的现代诗人之一,新超现实主义流派和"深度意象派"的代表人物之一。

【注释】
① 此诗 2008 年发表于《纽约客》(New Yorker)杂志第 35 期。Alba,西班牙语,意为"清晨"。
② terrace wall:阶梯状斜坡,这里指类似梯田的山坡。
③ almond:杏树。

第六章
诗歌与田园

【作品赏析】

　　威廉·斯坦利·默温是当代美国著名诗人,曾两获普利策诗歌奖,并于 2010 年成为美国第 17 位桂冠诗人。默温的诗歌中具备某种佛教的神秘气息,其作品往往如禅宗一般点到即止,多描述而少评论之语。此外,默温也是一位对大自然怀有特殊感情的诗人,他的诗歌中常体现出明显的生态意识。他喜爱描写田园风光,擅长捕捉自然界中微妙的细节,作品的整体风格清新自然。自 20 世纪 60 年代起,默温隐居在夏威夷岛上。据说,在那里,他拥有一片小树林,种植着世界上的一些濒危植物。也许,正是这种与自然、与田园的零距离接触极大地影响了默温的诗歌创作。

　　薄雾初升之时,诗人走在通向梯田般山坡的小道上,周围豆花绽放,在晨曦中清香四溢。一条小道蜿蜒在眼前,通向小山,诗人穿过橄榄树丛,走过繁花满树的杏林,身后隐约可见农家小屋升起的袅袅炊烟。一转身,他又闻到了豆花散发的淡淡香味,仿佛俏皮的小姑娘。移步向前,传来了骡子身上铃铛的响声。那骡蹄踩在田间的小石头上,发出清脆的声响。骡子的主人对着骡子轻声细语,仿佛在说着赞美它的话。走在半山腰的农夫和骡子仿佛行走在彩云之间。农夫哼着小曲,好像是专门在为骡子哼唱。他用农家方言旁若无人地哼着,他哼得投入,仿佛和自然融于一体。这低沉、有点陌生的曲调从不远处飘来,和清晨的小山、炊烟、树丛、晨曦、小径、豆花、花香、骡铃一并展现在诗人眼前,引发诗人无限的感慨。

　　在形式上,默温的诗歌多不加标点。在这首诗中,标点符号的省略更使得作品读起来像是穿行在一条林间小道上,也少了几分阻隔,使得读者感觉到流畅自然,一气呵成。从头至尾,读过之后,闭目深思,诗韵久久不散,也许这就是诗人的高明之处。全诗仅开头第一个单词"climbing"的首字母大写,给人的感觉是其后的所有词汇都由这一个词语顺带而出,这在视觉上也营造出整体合一的效果。在诗人的眼中,周围的一情一景、一草一木甚至包括农夫和骡子都是自然的一部分。反过来说,从"豆花"的角度来看,诗人又何尝不是自然的一份子呢?"where suddenly the scent of the bean flowers found me"这一句颇具俏皮之意,既把豆花的可爱呈现了出来,又使得诗人本身也成为自然的"眼中之物",不知不觉中与自然融于一体。

描写田园的诗歌多用词简单,默温的这一首《清晨》尤甚。简练的用词和诗中描写的清晨、薄雾、小山、晨光、树丛、花香、农夫、骡子以及用方言哼唱出的小曲等在整体的感觉上相得益彰。读此诗,读者恍若被诗人带入了一幅中国的山水写意画卷,简简单单的几笔,仿佛不经意的泼墨挥洒,却将大自然的美展现得淋漓尽致。

小 结

以田园为主题的诗歌,将人类赖以生存的大自然作为描述对象。诗人通过诗歌的形式展现大自然,一方面,是对诗人所处时代的自然环境和山水田园风貌的记录。通过诵读这些不朽的诗作,读者可以跨过时间和地域上的限制,通过诗人的引导,加上自我的想象,对某一种自然的存在进行还原;另一方面,除了对自然的忠实的描写,很多诗人又在字里行间引申出对人生、对社会的思考。也就是说,自然本身就有一种"净化"能力,诗人通过亲身感受自然,心灵得到净化和升华,思索出人生的道理。通过诗歌,诗人又将这些思考的结晶记录下来,读者读后产生思索和共鸣,这又使得诗歌的寓意更加深刻。也就是说,描写自然田园的诗多是"托物言志",通过对自然景物的描述,诗人生发出一系列的思考,从而帮助读者了解人生百态,对人生的苦难表达同情,对成功与失败、对与错、是与非进行积极的思索。

第六章
诗歌与田园

以田园为主题的诗歌也反映了人类为了生存所要处理的多重关系中的一种：人与自然的关系。在人类历史上，人与自然的关系曾长期被忽视。反映人类高度文明的工业化进程是以对自然造成的无可恢复的破坏为代价的。随着城市文明的发展，代表自然原始状态的乡村文明也在不断地衰落。这不仅表现在城市的不断扩大和乡村的不断萎缩上，更重要的在于人们对城市文明的向往和对乡村文明的疏离上。显然，在总体上城市化的进程（就目前情况而言）必然要挤压乡村文化的生存空间。虽然"回归自然"一度成为人们的向往，对很多人而言，真正的自然似乎只存在孩提时代亦真亦幻的记忆里。每一代人对自然的记忆都是不同的，而诗人的任务之一，就在于唤醒人类对自然本真状态的认识。

另外，诗人这一写作群体的审美态度和审美观点在田园诗中也得到了体现。自然是美的，美是可以抒发的，所以有了诗歌，所以有了田园诗。作为现代人，非常遗憾的一点是，人们往往失去了对美的认识。在流行文化日益盛行的今天，"审美"似乎成为了一种奢侈品。对于什么是"美"，很多人失去了应有的评判标准。在这种情况下，阅读田园诗有利于读者形成自我的审美标准。田园诗通过还原自然的本真状态，提醒读者自然的存在，呼吁读者有一双善于发现的眼睛，帮助读者从自然中发现美，从描述自然的艺术中发现美。

以上四首诗歌选自不同的时代，英国和美国诗人各占两位。两位英国诗人均是19世纪有名的诗人，以擅长描写自然景物见长。在 *The World Is Too Much with Us* 中，华兹华斯一反以往（如 *I Wandered Lonely as a Cloud* 中）开朗明快的节奏和对大自然的溢美之词，而是选取了另外一个角度，把目光聚焦于人类对自然和环境的轻视和破坏。该诗第一句就直接点出人类有负自然的美意，接下来的每一句都像是一记重锤敲打在读者的心上，表达出了诗人对人类生态环境恶化的担忧。*The Skylark* 虽同为描写自然景物的诗作,但是,有着"北安普顿农民诗人"之称的约翰·克莱尔,却把着眼点径直投向乡村的一草一木、空中的云雀和奔跑的孩童,通过一幅幅充满质感的画面,为读者呈上了一幕活灵活现的乡村风俗画。当然,他的目的并非简单地引导人们重温北安普敦的乡野生活。如果说华兹华斯的 *The World Is Too Much with Us* 发出的是冷峻的思考和严肃的拷问,那么,在 *The Skylark* 中,克莱尔则意在暗示生命的美好纯真以及生态循环往复的必然性。罗伯特·弗罗斯特和威廉·斯坦利·默温,前者是 20 世纪美国最受欢迎的诗人之一,后者也是当代美国极富声望的诗人。两人都是写作乡村题材诗歌的高手。其中,弗罗斯特尤以简洁的描写、凝练的语言和深刻的哲理而名重诗坛;默温的诗风清新秀丽,多直接描写景物而极少有主观的评论之语。*Stopping by Woods on a Snowy Evening* 是一般读者耳熟能详的一首诗,诗人前半部分重点营造出了雪夜树林宁谧的氛围,落雪之后的夜晚、覆满白雪的大地和树林、一人一马,以及在树林停留时诗人展开的想象。场景简单,但是全诗在前半部分做了大量铺垫,在最后一节又突转笔锋,以颇具哲理性的诗句收尾,意味深长。*ALBA* 一诗的标题本身就给人以一种清丽、脱俗的异国情致,全诗极力勾勒出一幅"乡村清晨"图,一景一物无不展现清晨的清新与秀丽,读过此诗有如沐春风之快意。简短的一首诗,似乎将读者带入了一个颇有异国风情的场景里。

　　相较于其他题材的诗歌而言,由于田园诗诗风清新,用词多简洁,场景描述也以朴素为主,所以对田园诗歌的欣赏相对而言比较简单。但是欣赏此类诗歌,要注意两点:一是要试图抓住诗人的思绪,力求顺着他的字词句所构建的画面发展自己的想象;二是要注意,很多描写田园的英美诗人尤擅长于"借景抒情"和"托物言志",在他们描摹的山水风光背后往往藏着深刻的哲学意蕴。对这种思维方式和创作方式的了解可以说也是把握英美诗歌的一把钥匙。以上四首诗歌,除了 *The World Is Too Much with Us* 直言不讳地展现人类对自然的破坏,呼吁关爱自然和生态(这也是为了更加直接地表述诗人的观点)之外,其他三首诗歌显得或多或少比较委婉和深藏不露,比较明显的是 *The Skylark* 和 *Stopping by Woods on a Snowy Evening*。*The Skylark* 包含的哲理性思考是多个层面上的,诗人由云雀被放学的孩子惊飞而引发思考。该诗的技巧在于,诗人没有直接表述,而是通过孩子们只看到云雀飞得高而羡慕却不知道云雀终究要飞落回来,落在地面上,这样就使读者不自觉地进行对照和思考。*Stopping by Woods on a Snowy Evening* 一诗延续弗罗斯特的风格,通过对日常事件的描写,转而以几句妙笔生花般的诗句点出生活中的哲理。ALBA 表面上看不出有"哲理性思考"的痕迹,其实这也是诗人的写作特色。在诗中,诗人未发一句评论和感叹,而是将重点放在刻画和描写周围的一草一木之中。其表现就如智者观物,倒是颇有几分禅宗的冥思默想。

  以上四首诗歌或直陈对生态的忧思,或由自然之物、自然之景升华出无限的哲理性思考,或擅长于对瑰丽乡村田园图景的刻画,从不同角度展现出了田园诗的魅力,颇有代表性。诚然,由于篇幅以及诗歌风格、诗人所处时代等的限制,我们只能姑且选取以上四首田园诗歌加以鉴赏。我们希望,一滴水可以折射出太阳的光辉,至少这些作品可以帮助读者对英美诗歌中颇有"田园风"和"乡土气息"的诗作有一个初步的认识。在本章的"扩展阅读篇目"的板块中,我们还列出了更多的作品,可供读者参考。在英美诗歌历史上,以自然景物描写见长的诗人有很多,比如为大家所熟知的莎士比亚、丁尼生、布莱克、彭斯、柯勒律治、骚赛、雪莱、济慈、梭罗、爱默生、惠特曼、狄金森等。到了 20 世纪，借助于生态文学研究的发展，田园诗更加引起评论界以及读者的关注。很多以描写乡村景致见长的诗人和诗作渐渐进入读者的视野，如罗宾逊·杰弗斯、加里·斯奈德、玛丽·奥利弗等。如果说 19 世纪以及 19 世纪之前的诗人更多钟情于自然写意，缺乏自觉的生态意识的话，那么，20 世纪很多的诗人则多数是在生态意识的引导下进行积极的创作。比如，罗宾逊·杰弗斯在其诗歌 *The Beauty of Things* 中曾有这样的表述：

... rock

And water and sky are constant — to feel

Greatly, and understand greatly, and express greatly the natural

Beauty, is the sole business of poetry.

扩展阅读篇目

To a Waterfowl by William Cullen Bryant

The Echoing Green by William Blake

To Daffodils by Robert Herrick

To Autumn by John Keats

Written at a Small Distance from My House by William Wordsworth

I Wandered Lonely as a Cloud by William Wordsworth

A Bird Came down the Walk by Emily Dickinson

Regarding Wave by Gary Snyder

The Wild Honey Suckle by Philip Frenau

第六章
诗歌与田园

Nothing Gold Can Stay by Robert Frost
After Apple-Picking by Robert Frost
This World by Mary Oliver

第七章

诗歌与政治

点 题

The opinion that art should have nothing to do with politics is itself a political attitude.

—— George Orwell

人们常说,文学就是人学。那么,诗学,自然也属于人学的范畴。不管是有心还是无意,自古以来,诗歌与政治往往纠缠在一起;或者从某种意义上来说,诗歌本身就是政治。在英国文学史上,诗人因其作品内容而导致命运急剧改变的事例可以举出很多。有人因为"政治准确"而得到当局的青睐,获得重用,官运亨通;也有人因为作品内容冒犯了国王或统治阶层而被投入监狱甚至身首异处;还有一些人,因为他们诗歌创作风格的变幻多姿,免不了要经历人生的大起大落、大喜大悲。以华兹华斯为例,谁都知道他是"湖畔派"诗人的代表,以吟唱风花雪月、鱼石鸟兽为其所长。但是,读一读他所写的两首关于伦敦的诗歌,我们会发现纯情如华兹华斯者有时也注定要在字里行间夹带进自己的思想、态度和倾向。他那著名的 *Composed upon Westeminster Bridge* 是一曲唱给伦敦城的赞歌,里面竭尽溢美之词。但是,在 *London*

第七章
诗歌与政治

1802 里,他呈现在我们面前的却完全是另一幅景象。伦敦城被比作死水一潭的绝望之地,诗人在一开始就声嘶力竭地呼唤早已逝去的弥尔顿重回人间,可见他对现实的极度失望和不满。这两首诗歌的创作时间同在 1802 年,但是,它们在内容上和思想感情上却出现了如此强烈的反差,个中原因恐怕与当时英国社会的政治气候有关,也与英国周边(特别是法国)的政治大环境有关,更与华兹华斯对时局的评判以及个人的好恶有关。再来说说差不多与华兹华斯同时代的雪莱,虽然出身高贵、才华横溢,诗人雪莱却无法见容于当时的英国主流社会,后来不得不远走他乡并导致他最终不幸溺水身亡。雪莱的悲剧无非在于他的直率和不肯妥协,他的作品言词犀利、锋芒毕露,矛头所指直逼权贵和统治阶级,怪不得他会遭到主导舆论的统治阶层的忌恨,把他视为异数。

就北美大陆来说,情形也是如此。早在独立战争时期,美国就曾涌现出了著名的革命诗人菲利普·弗瑞诺。他一方面充满热情地讴歌新大陆优美的自然风光,与此同时,又以诗歌为武器大胆地揭露英国殖民者的种种劣迹和暴行。他的诗歌为激励北美殖民地的人民奋起反击,争取自己的权利,并最终赢得民族独立斗争做出了特殊的贡献。又比如惠特曼,无论从哪个角度来看,他都是出类拔萃的。他的作品今天仍受到追捧,他的风格一直被他人所模仿,尤其需要指出的是,他诗歌中所倡导的民主、自由、平等和相互关爱的理念现在已差不多成为美国精神的代名词。可以说,他是新生的美利坚合众国最早、也是最积极的宣传者和歌颂者之一;而且,他的歌唱完全是发自内心,绝不带有丝毫功利的色彩。惠特曼的诗歌是艺术的,同时也是政治的。

进入 20 世纪以来,西方各国的社会政治经济发生了翻天覆地的变化。以美国为例,伴随着其国力的强盛以及国内各类社会矛盾的激化，政治这个概念的内涵也得到了延伸。所谓政治，已不再像过去那样简单地指涉政府以及政府的主要内外政策等。此刻，政治开始慢慢渗透到了社会生活的各个方面，反战、民权运动、女性主义、环境保护，甚至堕胎和婚姻等，由这些浪潮和运动所带来的诉求日益变成人们日常生活中活生生的政治。自然而然地，这一切的变化也在诗歌中找到了影子。于是，我们看到了更多不同面目的诗歌。以艾伦·金斯堡为代表的"垮掉派"诗人和小说家以不羁的笔触和狂热的调子对着美国发出了一声声"嚎叫"。还有罗伯特·潘·沃伦、约翰·克鲁·兰塞姆和艾伦·塔特等"南方逃逸派"诗人不合时宜的悲天悯人，他们除了悲壮就只剩下那忧伤的"南方联邦死难烈士颂歌"。还有查尔斯·奥尔森和他那著名的《投射体诗》以及在他主导下的"黑山派"诗人。还有罗伯特·洛厄尔、西尔维娅·普拉斯和安妮·塞克斯顿等人，他们或者是因为对现实的无奈，或者是因为不堪男权社会的压迫，从而选择走向了另一个极端——把自己的一切毫无保留地暴露在读者面前。还有格温多琳·布鲁克斯、玛雅·安吉罗、妮基·乔万尼等，她们是非洲裔女诗人的杰出代表，她们的歌唱更具有双重意义：既是为了种族的骄傲，也是为了女性的尊严。一言以蔽之，诗歌与政治的游戏始终在上演，诗歌与政治的游戏仍将继续上演。本章取名"诗歌与政治"，我们选取了英美两国四位具有代表性的诗人的重要作品，希望通过品读这些不朽名作，能够帮助读者就诗歌与政治之间的关系有一个初步的认识。

名篇导读

1. Song to the Men of England①
Percy Bysshe Shelley

1

Men of England, wherefore② plough
For the lords who lay ye③ low?
Wherefore weave with toil and care
The rich robes your tyrants wear?

2

Wherefore feed, and clothe, and save,
From the cradle to the grave④,
Those ungrateful drones⑤ who would
Drain your sweat — nay⑥, drink your blood?

3

Wherefore, Bees of England⑦, forge
Many a weapon, chain, and scourge⑧,
That these stingless drones may spoil⑨
The forced produce of your toil?

4

Have ye leisure, comfort, calm,
Shelter, food, love's gentle balm⑩?
Or what is it ye buy so dear
With your pain and with your fear?

5

The seed ye sow, another reaps⑪;
The wealth ye find, another keeps;
The robes ye weave, another wears;
The arms ye forge, another bears.

6

Sow seed—but let no tyrant reap;
Find wealth—let no impostor⑫ heap;
Weave robes—let not the idle wear;
Forge arms—in your defence to bear.

7

Shrink to your cellars, holes, and cells;
In halls ye deck another dwells.
Why shake the chains ye wrought⑬? Ye see
The steel ye tempered glance on ye⑭.

8

With plough and spade, and hoe and loom⑮,
Trace your grave, and build your tomb,
And weave your winding-sheet, till fair⑯
England be your sepulchre⑰.

【诗人简介】 珀西·比希·雪莱（Percy Bysshe Shelley, 1792—1822），英国浪漫主义诗人。代表作有《解放了的普罗米修斯》《致云雀》《西风颂》等。诗歌节奏明快、积极向上。

【注释】

① 此诗作于1819年秋。当时,雪莱曾拟将其印成传单广为散发,但因其内容激进导致无人敢承印。直至雪莱死后,此诗才得以发表。

② wherefore:古英语,为什么。

③ ye:古英语,你们,即英格兰人民。

④ From the cradle to the grave:直译为"从摇篮到坟墓",即指人的一生。

⑤ drone:雄蜂,这里喻指统治阶级和压榨老百姓的权贵。

⑥ nay:古英语,意为"不",用在此处意在层层递进、加强语气。

⑦ Bees of England:此处指受到剥削的广大劳动人民。

⑧ scourge:镣铐。

⑨ spoil:抢劫,掠夺。

⑩ balm:香脂,香油;有芳香味道的护手霜或润肤露等。

⑪ The seed ye sow, another reaps:英谚"As you sow, so will you reap"的变体,意思是说劳动者辛勤播下了种子,而收获(即不劳而获)的却是资本家和当权者。

⑫ impostor:骗子。

⑬ wrought:work过去式的一种,意为"锻造"。

⑭ The steel ye tempered glance on ye:意为"你们亲手锻造的钢铁现在却虎视眈眈地盯着你们"。

⑮ plough and spade, and hoe and loom:都是指耕作时所用的农具。

⑯ fair:美丽的。

⑰ sepulchre:坟墓。

【作品赏析】

珀西·比希·雪莱不仅是英国浪漫主义诗歌的旗手,还是一位颇有影响力的思想家和改革家。这首《致英格兰人民的歌》是雪莱最著名的政治抒情诗之一。1819 年 8 月初,英国曼彻斯特数万工人游行集会,要求改革和获得普选权,但遭到当局镇压,死伤数百人。远在意大利的雪莱接获李·亨特带来的不幸消息之后义愤填膺,写下了包括本诗在内的一系列作品,以示声援。由于这首诗言辞犀利、慷慨激昂,充满了战斗精神,特别是最后两节带有极大的鼓动性,因此,在当时很长一段时间内,出版商未敢承印。待到后来发表时,雪莱已去世十多年了。

本诗一开头就连问了几个"为什么",质问逆来顺受的英格兰人民为何甘于接受悲惨的现状?诗中写道,"英格兰人啊,你为何要给那些把你贬得一文不值的老爷辛勤耕作?你为何要给那些盗取锦衣玉食的暴君纺纱织布?你为何终日操劳,直到死去,仍心甘情愿让那些高高在上的强盗榨干你的血汗?英格兰的老百姓啊,你为何要打造出武器、锁链和镣铐,任由嗜血成性的暴徒夺走你的劳动所得?你们有闲暇时光,有惬意的那一刻吗?你们的房屋在哪里?还有食物?还有与亲密爱人分享的爱的礼物?如果这一切都没有你的份,那你们为何还要含辛茹苦?"这一连串的"为什么",层层推进、字字见血,把当时英国社会底层劳动者的艰辛和苦难描绘得淋漓尽致。接下来的第五小节,诗人对此前连篇的发问给出了直截了当的回答。他写道:"你们辛勤播种,却让别人来收获;你们创造财富,却不得不交给别人来保管;你们纺纱织布,却眼睁睁看着别人穿上华服;你们打造的武器,现在却落在他人的手里。"在第六小节,诗人语气陡转,态度变得更加果断决绝。他连着使用了四个祈使句,并且,词序和句子的顺序也和此前的第五小节一一对应。显然,在经过前四节振聋发聩的提问过后,诗人认为必须要付诸行动了。他大声高呼,呼吁英国的老百姓不要再逆来顺受,必须行动起来做自己命运的主人。在最后的两节中,诗人似乎是在向英国人民发出警告:如果你们再不觉醒,再不奋起反抗,再不敢挣脱身上的枷锁,那么,美丽的英格兰终将是埋葬你们的坟场。

这首诗歌目的明确,态度鲜明硬朗,总体的基调激越昂扬,具有极大的鼓动性。从创作的特色来看,全篇共八节,每节四行,以双行韵式 aabb 押韵,结构简单明晰,读来朗朗上口,易于被普通劳动者接受并传播。作品中,诗人多处使用巧妙的比喻,如把统治者比作"雄蜂"、"骗子"等,突出了诗人对他们的厌恶之情。此外,诗人还在作品中使用了大量的排比句,不但有效地渲染了气氛、强化了主题,也有助于作品在结构上显得更为流畅自然。

2. O Captain! My Captain![①]
Walt Whitman

O Captain! My Captain! our fearful trip[②] is done;
The ship has weathered every rack, the prize we sought is won;
The port is near, the bells I hear, the people all exulting[③],
While follow eyes the steady keel, the vessel grim and daring[④]:
But O heart! heart! heart!
O the bleeding drops of red,
Where on the deck my Captain lies,
Fallen cold and dead.

O Captain! my Captain! rise up and hear the bells;
Rise up—for you the flag is flung—for you the bugle trills⑤;
For you bouquets and ribbon'd wreaths⑥—for you the shores a-crowding;
For you they call, the swaying mass, their eager faces turning;
Here Captain! dear father!
This arm beneath your head;
It is some dream that on the deck,
You've fallen cold and dead.

My Captain does not answer, his lips are pale and still;
My father does not feel my arm, he has no pulse nor will;
The ship is anchor'd safe and sound, its voyage closed and done;
From fearful trip, the victor ship, comes in with object won;
Exult, O shores, and ring, O bells!
But I, with mournful tread⑦,
Walk the deck my Captain lies,
Fallen cold and dead.

【注释】

① captain：本意为"船长"，此处指美国第 16 任总统亚伯拉罕·林肯。林肯总统领导美国人民结束了内战，废除了奴隶制，而他本人却在这胜利和欢庆的时刻不幸遇刺身亡。这首诗是美国著名诗人沃尔特·惠特曼（Walt Whitman，1819—1892）为悼念林肯总统而作。

② fearful trip：这里是一种比喻的用法，指美国的南北战争。

③ exult:狂喜,欢欣鼓舞。

④ grim and daring:威严和英武的。

⑤ for you the bugle trills:人们为你吹响了号角。

⑥ ribbon'd wreaths:相当于 ribboned wreaths,花环。

⑦ tread:移步,踩踏。

【作品赏析】

  王佐良先生在评价19世纪晚期的美国诗歌时曾经说过:"惠特曼异军突起,用全新的内容和全新的艺术为英语诗歌开辟了一条新的大路,真所谓石破天惊。""石破天惊"的惠特曼堪称美国诗坛的一个传奇。他乐观开朗,充满自信,始终以满腔的热情为脚下这片神奇的土地引吭高歌。他的诗是热烈的、蓬勃向上的。就创作技巧而言,惠特曼也走在了时代的前列。他独树一帜,创立了自由体诗歌,还把大量日常用语引入诗歌,为诗歌走向大众迈出了一大步。

  这首《哦,船长,我的船长》是惠特曼诗歌体系中比较特殊的一个作品,它是诗人为了纪念遇刺身亡的林肯总统而作的一首挽歌,或者说,它也是一首颂歌,是对已故总统建立的丰功伟绩表达敬意的一曲颂歌。

  诗歌开篇把林肯总统比作船长,带领着美国这艘大船在海上无畏地航行。大船威武雄壮,正徐徐驶入港口,在喧闹的鼓乐声中,岸上的人们翘首以待,一片欢欣鼓舞的场面。险恶的航程终于结束,胜利已经到来。然而,就在此时,一句"O heart! heart! heart!"猝然使人心碎。接踵而至的"the bleeding drops of red"使人们明白了现实的残酷:伟大的船长没有死在惊涛骇浪之中,却倒在了这欢庆胜利的时刻。诗人连用了两个"O"和三个感叹号,表达了极度的震惊和难以言说的悲痛心情。最后一句,"他倒下了,已死去,已冰凉"与此前人们的欢腾场景形成强烈反差,由大喜跌入大悲。第二节开始,诗人仍不能相信船长已死,他希望林肯总统能醒过来,能站起来看看人声鼎沸的庆祝场面。港口彩旗招展,鼓乐声声,热情欢呼的人们手捧着鲜花涌向胜利归来的英雄。尽管他们的船长、美国的国父林肯总统躺倒在甲板上,浑身冰冷一动不动,而"我"却仍在不停地呼唤他的名字。在第三节的头两行,"我"终于不得不承认:船长没有说话,他双唇惨白而安静,没有了脉搏和生命的迹象。至此,"我"再也无法控制自己的情绪,巨大的悲伤再次袭来。"我"想到了航行途中的艰难险阻,想到了胜利的来之不易,面对岸上万众欢庆的场面,"我"只能拖着沉重的脚步从船长冰冷的身旁缓缓走过。

　　这首诗共有三节,每节八行,前四行是双韵体,后四行是民歌体,韵式为 aabbcded,属于典型的传统格律诗,与惠特曼擅长的自由体诗形成了极大的反差。从诗行的安排来看,四个长句加上四个短句组成的诗节在外形上酷似远航归来的大船,也巧妙地呼应了全诗的主题。此外,这首诗歌中对于传统修辞手法的妙用可以说达到了化境。首先,是隐喻的运用,从标题开始一直到全篇结束,我们看到的是两个赫然在目的形象:大船和船长。第二,是排比句式的运用,三个诗节中多处出现短促有力的句子,如此循环往复,绵延不绝,大大增强了作品的悲剧效果。第三,是反复手法的运用。比如,连续在三个小节末尾出现的"Fallen cold and dead"就是一例。第四,是呼语(apostrophe)的使用。从一开始的"O Captain! My Captain! our fearful trip is done",到第二小节开头的"O Captain! my Captain! rise up and hear the bells",一直到第三节的"Exult, O shores, and ring, O bells!"等等,"我"先是满怀深情地呼唤船长,仿佛船长真能听到这一切并能站起来和大家一道欢庆胜利。待到后来,"我"终于明白船长已不可能醒来,于是,"我"转而对着岸上的人群呼唤,请求他们为死去的船长奏乐、欢呼,以此表达对船长最后的敬意。第五,是成对词的运用。比如,grim and daring, cold and dead, pale and still, safe and sound, closed and done 等,它们对于强化全篇庄重肃穆的气氛作用明显。最后,是音响效果的制造。除了遵循相应的韵式以外,这首诗歌还多处使用了押头韵(alliteration),比如,flag is flung, safe and sound 等。总之,这是一首打动人心的经典之作,虽然通篇弥漫着挥散不去的伤感和失落,但同时也透出几许壮怀激烈的气概。这是一首悼亡诗,更可以被看作是一部歌颂自由和民主的宣言书。

3. Her Kind①

Anne Sexton

I have gone out, a possessed② witch,
haunting the black air, braver at night;
dreaming evil, I have done my hitch③
over the plain houses, light by light:
lonely thing, twelve-fingered, out of mind.
A woman like that is not a woman, quite.
I have been her kind.

I have found the warm caves in the woods,
filled them with skillets④, carvings, shelves,
closets, silks, innumerable goods;

fixed the suppers for the worms and the elves⑤:
whining, rearranging the disaligned⑥.
A woman like that is misunderstood.
I have been her kind.

I have ridden in your cart, driver,
waved my nude arms at villages going by,
learning the last bright routes, survivor
where your flames still bite my thigh
and my ribs crack where your wheels wind.
A woman like that is not ashamed to die.
I have been her kind.

【诗人简介】安妮·塞克斯顿(Anne Sexton, 1928—1974), 美国"自白派"诗人。生前曾患有精神病, 诗歌创作对她是一种治疗和复活。她的诗敏锐有力, 1967年因诗集《生或死》获得普利策奖。

【注释】

① 此诗选自美国"自白派"女诗人安妮·塞克斯顿于1960年出版的诗集《去精神病院中途而归》(To Bedlam and Part Way Back)。

② possessed: 被(妖魔、情欲等)迷住的或缠住的。

③ I have done my hitch: 此处的 hitch 指在黑夜里从屋顶一跃而过, 因此, 全句的意思可理解为"我完成了这个壮举。"

④ skillet: 煮锅, 平底煎锅。

⑤ elves: elf 的复数形式, 意为"精灵"。

⑥ rearranging the disaligned：把混乱的东西重新放整齐。

【作品赏析】

"自白派"诗人以大胆、无所顾忌和赤裸以对的坦诚而出名,他们追求最大程度地把自己的生存状态、生活经历和情感体验等不加修饰地呈现出来以引起读者的共鸣。安妮·塞克斯顿也不例外,在这首《她那一类》中,她就发出了独出心裁的另类声音:要成为遭社会所不齿和唾弃的那一类人物。

诗歌开篇刻画了一个被魔法缠身的女巫形象,她身披黑色斗篷,骑着长把扫帚,习惯在黑夜里腾空而起,从一家房顶漂移到另一家房顶。她长着十二根手指,梦想着干一些坏事。但是,在黑夜出没的女巫其实也有自己的心酸,她的孤独源自她的与众不同。她完全不是一个普通的家庭妇女,满足于每天辛勤料理家务、相夫教子。接下里的一句"A woman like that is not a woman, quite"则清楚地表明这样的一个女人与社会的期待相距太远,是不可能为社会所接纳的。出人意料的是,在最后一句,诗人果敢地喊出了"I have been her kind"。没有躲闪,没有犹豫,她的特立独行的叛逆性格由此展露无遗。第二节的视角转向了森林里的洞穴,这里有女巫温暖的家。她为这个家添置了锅瓢、雕刻品、搁架、壁橱和丝绸,把一切整理得井然有序,她甚至还为虫子和精灵准备晚餐。这里的描述展示了女巫贤惠能干的一面,也显示了她柔性的一面。原来她并非人们唯恐避之不及的怪物,她也有生活的品位,也懂得如何勤俭持家和体贴照顾他人。只不过,除此之外,她还希望拥有更多其他的追求。而在所谓"正常"的家庭里,这却是一个永远无法实现的愿望。于是,她只能选择逃离,即便这意味着必须承受世人的误解。"A woman like that is misunderstood"这样的句子读来虽然令人心痛,却真实地道出了女巫的倔犟和不妥协。到了最后一节,女巫的态度变得更加清晰和硬朗。她对于自己选择挑战所谓正统的社会规范感到无怨无悔,就算"大腿被熊熊的火焰灼伤",就算"肋骨遭到坚硬车轮的碾压",她也在所不惜。她要坚持做一回真的自我,她不甘心只是充当配角或成为男权社会的附庸。她并不怕死,相反,她倒愿意为了自己的理想而轰轰烈烈地死去。

  这首诗歌共分三节,每节七行,韵律齐整、规范。每一小节的首行都以"I have ..."的句式开头,简单清晰明了,把一个勇敢、率真和具有强悍叛逆性格的女性形象刻画得灵动逼真。而在每一节的末尾,诗人也以相同的"I have been her kind"作为结束,既照应题目,也有助于突出诗人的态度。作为出自"自白派"诗人的代表性作品,这首《她那一类》书写的不仅仅是个人的遭遇,更代表了女性作为一个群体所发出的抗议和呐喊。因此,从某种意义上来说,这是一曲女性主义的自白书和宣言书。

4. America[①]

Allen Ginsberg

America I've given you all and now I'm nothing.
America two dollars and twenty seven cents January 17, 1956.
I can't stand my own mind.
America when will we end the human war[②]?
Go fuck yourself with your atom bomb.
I don't feel good don't bother me.
I won't write my poem till I'm in my right mind.

America when will you be angelic③?

When will you take off your clothes?

When will you look at yourself through the grave?

When will you be worthy of your million Trotskyites④?

America why are your libraries full of tears?

America when will you send your eggs to India⑤?

I'm sick of your insane demands.

When can I go into the supermarket and buy what I need with my good looks?

America after all it is you and I who are perfect not the next world.

Your machinery is too much for me.

You made me want to be a saint.

There must be some other way to settle this argument.

Burroughs is in Tangiers⑥ I don't think he'll come back it's sinister.

Are you being sinister or is this some form of practical joke?

I'm trying to come to the point.

I refuse to give up my obsession.

America stop pushing I know what I'm doing.

America the plum blossoms⑦ are falling.

I haven't read the newspapers for months, everyday somebody goes on trial for murder.

America I feel sentimental about the Wobblies⑧.

America I used to be a communist when I was a kid and I'm not sorry.

I smoke marijuana every chance I get.

I sit in my house for days on end and stare at the roses in the closet.

When I go to Chinatown I get drunk and never get laid.

My mind is made up there's going to be trouble.

You should have seen me reading Marx.

My psychoanalyst thinks I'm perfectly right.

I won't say the Lord's Prayer.

I have mystical visions and cosmic vibrations.

America I still haven't told you what you did to Uncle Max⑨ after he came over from Russia.

I'm addressing you.

Are you going to let our emotional life be run by *Time Magazine*?

I'm obsessed by *Time Magazine*.

I read it every week.

Its cover stares at me every time I slink past the corner candystore.

I read it in the basement of the Berkeley Public Library.

It's always telling me about responsibility. Businessmen are serious.

Movie producers are serious. Everybody's serious but me.

It occurs to me that I am America.

I am talking to myself again.

Asia is rising against me.

第七章
诗歌与政治

I haven't got a chinaman's chance.

I'd better consider my national resources.

My national resources consist of two joints of marijuana millions of genitals

an unpublishable private literature that goes 1400 miles and hour and

twenty-five-thousand mental institutions.

I say nothing about my prisons nor the millions of underprivileged who live in

my flowerpots under the light of five hundred suns.

I have abolished the whorehouses of France, Tangiers is the next to go.

My ambition is to be President despite the fact that I'm a Catholic.

America how can I write a holy litany in your silly mood?

I will continue like Henry Ford⑩ my strophes are as individual as his

automobiles more so they're all different sexes

America I will sell you strophes $2500 apiece $500 down on your old strophe

America free Tom Mooney⑪

America save the Spanish Loyalists⑫

America Sacco & Vanzetti⑬ must not die

America I am the Scottsboro boys⑭.

America when I was seven momma took me to Communist Cell meetings they

sold us garbanzos a handful per ticket a ticket costs a nickel and
 the
speeches were free everybody was angelic and sentimental about
 the
workers it was all so sincere you have no idea what a good thing
 the party
was in 1835 Scott Nearing was a grand old man a real mensch
 Mother
Bloor made me cry I once saw Israel Amter plain. Everybody
 must have
been a spy.
America you don't really want to go to war.
America it's them bad Russians.
Them Russians them Russians and them Chinamen. And them
 Russians.
The Russia wants to eat us alive. The Russia's power mad. She
 wants to take
our cars from out our garages.
Her wants to grab Chicago. Her needs a Red Reader's Digest.
 her wants our
auto plants in Siberia. Him big bureaucracy running our
 fillingstations.
That no good. Ugh. Him makes Indians learn read. Him need
 big black niggers.
Hah. Her make us all work sixteen hours a day. Help.
America this is quite serious.

第七章
诗歌与政治

America this is the impression I get from looking in the
  television set.
America is this correct?
I'd better get right down to the job.
It's true I don't want to join the Army or turn lathes in precision
  parts
factories, I'm nearsighted and psychopathic anyway.
America I'm putting my queer shoulder to the wheel.

【诗人简介】艾伦·金斯堡(Allen Ginsberg, 1926—1997),美国诗人,"垮掉的一代"之父。《诗集 1947—1980》收录了其所有重要诗作,其风格继承了英国诗人威廉·布莱克及惠特曼的传统。

【注释】
① 此诗由美国诗人艾伦·金斯堡于 1956 年在加州伯克利所作,后被收入他的《嚎叫及其他诗歌集》(Howl and Other Poems)。

② the human war:这里是一种反讽的手法,事实上,凡是战争都不可能是人道的。

③ angelic:天使般的。

④ Trotskyites:托洛茨基主义者。20 世纪初在俄国工人运动中出现的反对列宁主义的机会主义者,以托洛茨基为其代表。

⑤ America when will you send your eggs to India:据史料记载,1943 年印度发生大饥荒,民众饿死不计其数。此处金斯堡似乎在质问美国为何不能慷慨解囊,向遭受饥荒的印度伸出援手。

⑥ Burroughs is in Tangiers:威廉·巴勒斯(William Burroughs)是金斯堡的亲密战友、"垮掉派"的重要成员,代表作为

小说《赤裸的午餐》，他因从墨西哥非法运输毒品曾被美国政府流放。

⑦ plum blossoms：梅花，喻指中国。

⑧ the Wobblies：the Industrial Workers of the World 的别称，即世界产业工人联合会。

⑨ Uncle Max：指金斯堡的舅父 Max Livergant，系从俄罗斯移民美国的犹太裔社会主义者。

⑩ Henry Ford：美国汽车大王，福特汽车公司的创立者。

⑪ Tom Mooney：美国 20 世纪初工运领袖，曾度过 22 年的牢狱生涯，后于 1936 年获得释放。

⑫ Spanish Loyalists：在西班牙内战期间，美国因其国内的《中立法》而采取了纵容佛朗哥法西斯统治的政策，助长了右翼集团的势力。

⑬ Sacco & Vanzetti：萨科和范塞蒂，意大利无政府主义者。1927 年，两人因美国马萨诸塞州一宗劫杀案而被判处死刑。当时舆论认为，他们的罪名成立是因其无政府主义信仰，因而得不到公正的审判。1977 年，马萨诸塞州州长为两人平反。

⑭ Scottsboro boys：1931 年，9 名黑人青少年于阿拉巴马州的斯科茨伯勒市法院被控强奸两名白人少女，在证据不足的情况下，四人被判罪名成立，其中一人被处死，三人入狱，入狱者中有一人在狱中被狱警枪杀。

【作品赏析】

要读懂《美国》这首诗，首先必须要了解金斯堡其人。艾伦·金斯堡的名字早已被人们贴上了各种标签，他曾在哥伦比亚大学求学，也曾在精神病院待过；他热衷于吸食大麻，强烈主张同性恋，

第七章
诗歌与政治

同时却提倡信仰佛教的禅宗并修行禅定;他卷入过民权运动,反对战争,对美国政府进行过猛烈的抨击,还参加过多次示威游行。当然,他最主要的身份是"垮掉派"诗人。作为"垮掉派"的主将,他的一曲《嚎叫》当年以惊世骇俗的冲击力给美国文学界乃至整个美国社会制造了巨大的轰动效应,并曾被贬为淫秽作品。可以说,金斯堡的影响力不仅仅局限于诗歌的范畴。他是美国1960年代反主流文化的急先锋,是"垮掉派"成员中最彻底的无政府主义"脱俗者",他的声望甚至远及欧洲、亚洲和南美洲的一些国家。

《美国》一诗创作于1956年,后被选入于同年出版的《嚎叫及其他诗歌集》,是诗人的代表性作品之一。这首诗歌是在美国社会危机重重的背景下创作的,当时朝鲜战争刚刚结束,原子弹的阴影尚未散去,冷战以及和前苏联的太空军备竞赛正愈演愈烈;另一方面,美国国内的红色恐怖以及由此催生的麦卡锡主义也大行其道,民权运动风起云涌,物质至上和享乐主义盛行。在这首诗歌中,金斯堡以大无畏的勇气,结合"垮掉派"诗人的异质禀赋,向着一切他所鄙视和无法接受的社会现实发出了狂吼和嚎叫。他把目标对准了他的国家——美国,认为美国已经面目全非、彻底堕落。他抨击时政,高谈阔论战争与和平,揭开人道主义的疮疤和道德的沦落,嬉笑怒骂,无所不用其极。他还指控美国毁灭了它的人民,毁灭了人民的日常生活,毁灭了他们的梦想。这是一首旨趣不凡的政治诗,是对于美国政府的一纸无情的控告状。同时,这也是一首极其个人化的诗歌。全诗以第一人称贯穿始终,犹如一个清醒的疯子的内心独白,里面甚至还提到了诗人对大麻的迷恋、同性恋以及他和共产主义的关系等。这首诗歌通篇充满了愤怒的质问,情绪几近失控的边缘。这里有狂躁、失落、愤怒、谩骂以及痛哭流涕的哀嚎,这里有看似东拉西扯的装疯弄傻,但这里也有真情告白和一颗拳拳的赤子之心。

从表现手法来看，这首诗也体现了金斯堡一贯的风格。首先，是诗行的长度。金斯堡主张以意思的表达或意象的构建来决定诗句的安排，一般长句较多，这首诗也不例外。其次，是诗歌的语言。金斯堡受到惠特曼和威廉斯（William Carlos Williams）一脉的影响，语言多平实简单，绝无过分修饰之笔。在《美国》一诗中，为了呼应主题、宣泄情感，全篇的语言不但显得通俗和口语化，甚至有时不乏庸俗和粗俗。比如，"Go fuck yourself with your atom bomb"就是一个例子。一个 fuck 足以一吐诗人心中的愤懑之情，强烈影射了他对美国政府穷兵黩武的抗议和不满。第三，是拟人、隐喻、反讽和典故等传统修辞手段的有效使用。诗歌开篇，诗人即直抒胸臆，对着拟人化了的美国大声疾呼："美国，我把一切都给了你，现在我什么都不是"，表达出了战后一代人迷惘、困惑和精神上的极度失落。在第四行中，诗人首次开始了他对美国的质问，他写道，"美国，我们什么时候才能结束这人道的战争？"这里的"人道"一词是明显的反讽，也是对美国政府战争宣传的强力反击。因为，诗人相信凡是战争就必定是邪恶的。反讽的例子还有很多，比如，在诗歌的后半部分，诗人说"美国，你并不是真的想要打仗，是俄国佬，还有中国人……"等等。此外，在第十二和第二十五行，诗人分别写道，"美国，为什么你的图书馆里都是泪水？"和"美国，梅花凋落了"。这两个都是隐喻的例子，前者暗示在美国的土地上已找不到自由表达思想的地方，它不过是物欲横流、思想僵化的代名词罢了；而后者的"梅花"意象别具特色，似乎在叹息美国作为世界大国的地位正在下降，而东方的中国正悄然崛起。

总之，《美国》一诗可以被看作是在特定历史条件下的一部绝对另类的作品。它以逆潮流而动的气概、反常规的诗歌法则，为美国的文学界乃至整个美国社会投下了一枚重磅炸弹。当然,需要加以注意的是,这部作品中也透露出一个信息,那就是诗人对美国并没有彻底绝望。他的收尾的一句"America I'm putting my queer shoulder to the wheel"似乎在告诉人们他对美国仍怀有希望。而且更为重要的是,他那狂野的呐喊在当时也得到了人们积极的回应。琴斯·劳米斯洛斯在给艾伦·金斯堡的一首诗中就有这样的句子,"我羡慕你反叛十足的勇气,充满激情的言辞,预言家般狂烈的诅咒……"

小 结

　　文学不是独立于社会生活之外的,它记录着时代的变迁、沧海桑田,无论是国家处于风平浪静的发展期,还是人民生活在水深火热之中,作家和诗人都以高度的历史责任感抒写对生活的期待或者绝望。纵观英美文学发展史,诗人们始终牢牢准确地抓住时代发展的脉搏,以我心写真情,以真情映现实,那些与政治紧密联系的诗歌根植于社会大背景中,标志着诗人们与时俱进,反映社会变迁的勇气。

　　在本章中,我们从浩瀚的诗歌海洋中撷取了四首优秀作品来赏析。先是英国的积极浪漫主义诗人雪莱的《致英格兰人民的歌》。浪漫主义运动是英国工业革命和法国大革命共同作用下的产物,它反对古典主义的理性,注重个人情感的抒发。雪莱深受此思想影响,以一首气势磅礴、振奋人心的《致英格兰人民的歌》道出了资本主义剥削的本质,鼓舞了后来的欧洲工人运动和民族解放运动。第二篇《哦,船长,我的船长!》是美国诗人惠特曼为悼念林肯总统而写下的著名诗篇。林肯是美国第16任总统,他为维护国家统一、消除蓄奴制而领导了南北战争,解放了黑人奴隶。就在美国人民欢庆胜利的时刻，反动势力雇佣的刺客杀害了他。惠特曼为此极度悲痛，写下了多首诗纪念这位伟大的英雄，这首诗是其中最著名的。诗人以悲壮的基调，运用了比喻和象征的手法，把美国比作一艘航船，把林肯总统比作船长，把维护国家的统一和废奴斗争比作一段艰险的航程，透视了美国内战刚刚结束时各种矛盾交锋的场景。20世纪20年代，美国诗歌流派纷呈，安妮·塞克斯顿作为"自白诗"的代表，结合自身精神疾病的状况和治疗过程，创作的主题包括疯狂、欺骗、死亡等。她在最喜欢的诗《她那一类》中勇敢地剖析了痛苦的自我，深入探究了女性在真实的自我和传统观念中挣扎的困境。这与20世纪风起云涌的女权主义运动遥相呼应，关注女性成长与妇女解放。《美国》是"垮掉派"大师艾伦·金斯堡的不朽杰作，这位反文化的开拓者也是一位新文化的探索者。"垮掉派"运动一直被视作破坏艾森豪威尔与尼克松总统时期所创建的价值观的运动，金斯堡却认为此运动的主题超越了政治反抗的对与错，所做的都是出于一种脱离世俗的反叛的爱。在《美国》一诗中，诗人把美国当作自己曾经的密友，相信它的美好前景，相信一切自由民主都能得以实现，可是现实却摧毁了他的信任。这首诗生动地传达了战后一代人的感受，尤其是他们的智力和思想受到了深深的欺骗和无情的打击。

扩展阅读篇目

I, too, Sing America by Langston Hughes
If We Must Die by Claude McKay
Phenomenal Woman by Maya Angelou
Common Dust by Georgia Douglas Johnson
The Village by R. S. Thomas

第七章
诗歌与政治

Let America Be America Again by Langston Hughes
Housewife by Anne Sexton
Howl by Allen Ginsberg
Projective Verse by Charles Olson
America by Robert Creeley
I Know why the Caged Bird Sings by Maya Angelo
The Mother by Gwendolyn Brooks
The Love that Dares to Speak Its Name by James Kirkup

第八章

另类的诗歌

点 题

> *I could no more define poetry than a terrier can define a rat.*
>
> —— A. E. Housman

诗歌是世界上最古老的文学样式,迄今已走过了几千年的演变和发展历程。同时,诗歌作为一种高雅的文学艺术,也一直被奉为文学中的"贵族"。尽管关于诗歌的定义和理解不尽相同,但是,长期以来人们还是形成了某些共识。比如,诗歌常常被认为是反映社会生活的一面镜子,它倾注了作者强烈的思想和情感。此外,诗歌作品还呈现出一些共同的特征。例如,第一,诗歌是想象的产物,离开了丰富的想象,诗歌就无从谈起。第二,诗歌的结构比较严谨,往往遵循一定的规律。第三,诗歌讲究意在言外,因此语言多简洁、精炼。第四,诗歌具有鲜明的节奏、和谐的音韵、富于音乐美。这些特征构成了传统诗歌的基本要素,无论中西,莫不如此。不过,诗歌并非一成不变,随着时代的发展,诗歌的面貌也在不断发生改变。以活跃在19世纪中晚期的美国诗人惠特曼为例,他写的就是自由体诗歌,没有固定的韵脚,语言也是来自日常生活。再

第八章
另类的诗歌

比如,在1919年,著名诗人兼诗歌理论家艾略特在他的《传统与个人天赋》中曾提出了著名的"非个人化"理论。他强调,诗歌创作并不是要表现诗人的个性。在整个过程中,诗人仅仅是艺术表现的特殊工具,种种的印象和经验借助于诗人的心灵用意想不到的方式相互组合,于是就形成了诗。换言之,诗人的心灵只是一种贮藏器,收纳了无数种感觉、词句、意象等,它们潜藏在那儿,直到能组合成新化合物的各个分子都到齐,心灵的催化作用才开始发生作用,诗歌便产生了。因此,诗的产生实际上是一个冶炼、化合的非个性化过程。

当然,惠特曼也好,艾略特也罢,他们对于诗歌的改革或创新毕竟还在正常的诗歌范围之内,他们所写的诗歌也仍然是人们期待的模样。不过,环顾英美诗坛,另有一批诗人,其对待诗歌的态度以及对诗歌的处理方式却别有一番意趣,甚至可以说相当另类。这些诗人因受到环境的制约或出于特殊的癖好,在写作之时,多倾向于引入更多超常规的实验性元素。他们不屑于传统诗歌要素的羁绊,尤其注重创作中的个性与自由度。他们有的强调即兴性和随意性,有的刻意突出作品的外观结构,有的以追求极致的音乐效果为最大目标,还有的则致力于打通多种不同艺术门类之间的隔阂并试图将它们融会贯通在自己的作品里,并以此自得其乐。这种时尚、前卫的创作风格在一定程度上偏离了诗歌最初的轨迹,给人以一种娱乐诗歌、消遣诗歌的另类感觉。不过,必须承认,这样的尝试实际上古已有之。而且,越是到近代和现代,愈加呈现出旺盛的势头。之所以出现这样的趋向,一是和诗人个人的生活经历以及他们的美学追求不无关系。另外一个原因,则是社会政治经济文化大环境的影响使然。以美国为例,进入20世纪50年代中后期以后,由于国内外形势的急剧变化,大多数诗人和评论家已经开始对艾略特和新批评派所确立的美学原则感到疲倦。那些不安于现状的第二代和第三代诗人意识到原来封闭型的艺术形式已不能适应时代的要求,因此纷纷开始寻找新的富于弹性的表现样式,以便更加精确地反映新时代的社会生活和个人经验。于是乎,诗歌也从文学皇冠上的明珠一跃而下,变身成为了可供消遣与消费的特殊产品。诗歌或许仍然是高雅的,但它同时也是通俗的和触手可及的。更为有趣的是,诗歌不再是过去那种单纯的文字游戏,音乐、绘画、雕塑,甚至摄影也和诗歌走到了一起。以"纽约派"诗歌为例,受法国诗歌和绘画的影响,这一派诗人对超现实主义和达达派艺术兴趣浓厚。他们的创作追求支离破碎的完美,追求一种在荒诞不经的表象之下的和谐和契合。他们强调非写实性、抽象拼贴、口语(甚至俚语)化和荒诞幽默的倾向,因此,他们的诗歌有时看起来或听起来根本不像诗歌。《凸面镜的自画像》是"纽约派"诗人约翰·阿什贝里的代表作,这部作品的语言运用与传统诗歌的表达方式大相径庭,其中文雅词汇、日常用语以及俗语套话的穿插安排给人的感觉就好像是抽象派绘画或拼贴画中的颜色和材料一样扎眼。但是,这也是一种诗歌,虽然有点卖弄技巧的感觉,有点特立独行,有点为写诗而写诗的味道,可它照样受到读者的追捧。

  诗歌创作中超越常规的前卫实验还有很多,我们不能简单地以"好"或"坏"来加以标记。应该说,这些另类的诗歌形式拓宽了诗歌的路子,也给读者带来了新颖和奇特的阅读体验。在本章中,我们为大家挑选了四位诗人的作品,其中玛丽·柯勒律治基本应被归入19世纪诗人的行列。其他的三位诗人中,桑德堡是一般读者所熟悉的,只不过,他的这首《爵士幻想曲》此前恐较少为人所知。伯恩斯坦是美国当代著名的语言诗人,而伯福德的知名度相对略低,但他的《圣诞树》确是值得一读的好诗。

名篇导读

1. Slowly①

Mary Coleridge

Heavy is my heart,
Dark are thine② eyes.
Thou and I must part
Ere③ the sun rise.

Ere the sun rise
Thou and I must part.
Dark are thine eyes,
Heavy is my heart.

【诗人简介】玛丽·伊丽莎白·柯勒律治(Mary Elizabeth Coleridge,1861—1907),英国小说家、诗人,曾以 Anodos 的笔名写诗,受迪克森(Richard Watson Dixon)和罗塞蒂(Christina Rossetti)影响较多,一些作品(如 The Blue Bird 和 Thy Hand in Mine)曾被谱成曲。

【注释】

① 此诗由英国诗人兼小说家和散文作家玛丽·柯勒律治(Mary Coleridge,1861—1907)所作。

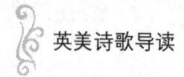

② thine：相当于 your，即"你的"，第三行中的 thou 相当于 you。

③ ere：古英语，在……之前。

【作品赏析】

　　回文，有时也称为"回文体"，是一种使用词序回环往复的修辞方法。而回文诗即是一种按一定规律将字词排列成文，回环往复都能诵读的诗。这种诗的形式变化多姿，能上下颠倒读，能顺读、倒读、斜读，也能交互读，等等，只要循着相应的规律，总能串联成优美的诗篇，可谓十分有趣而生动活泼。比如，有一副对联这样写道："清波碧水春归燕，细雨红窗晚落花。"此联工整有韵，清新俊逸。但你若倒过来读，则又别有一番情致："花落晚窗红雨细，燕归春水碧波清。"不仅平仄对仗工整，依然诗意浓郁，这就是回文诗的魅力所在。回文诗不仅在中国古典诗词中是一枝鲜艳夺目的奇葩，在英语诗歌创作中也不乏经典的例子，有则墓志铭是这样写的：

　　　　Shall we all die?

　　　　We shall die all；

　　　　All die shall we——

　　　　Die all we shall.

　　这是一首以单词为单位的回文诗，表面上看起来有点玩弄文字的嫌疑，但是细细揣摩，还是能感受到作者的良苦用心。回文诗重在一个"回"字，也难在一个"回"字，其成功与否，全在"回"的功夫上。回文可回在单词上，也可回在句子上。

　　玛丽·柯勒律治的这首《慢慢地》就是以句子为单位进行回文的诗作。这首小诗前四行正序排列，后四行倒序排列，首尾衔接，回环反复。诗中写道："我的心情悲戚，你的眼神忧郁，你我必须别离,赶在日出之时。"诗的第一行的"heavy"与第二行的"dark",一个沉郁,一个黯淡,两个字排列在一起;眼睛是心灵的窗户,"eyes"与"heart"的呼应,一副悲戚伤感的画面呈现在读者面前。后一诗节以前一诗节的最后一句作为开头,然后依次将第一节的四行倒序排列,相同的诗句,循环往复,恋人离别之时的那种依恋和难分难舍的情景表现得淋漓尽致,真可谓"多情自古伤离别!"一首仅有17个单词的小诗,以回文的形式呈现给读者,不仅形式上新颖独特,情感表达上也更深一层,与普通诗歌相比,多了一份情感的"迂回"之美。玛丽·柯勒律治出自名门之后,她的曾祖叔父是著名的浪漫主义诗人塞缪尔·泰勒·柯勒律治(Samuel Taylor Coleridge),她的诗歌也曾被英国桂冠诗人布列吉斯(Robert Bridges)评价为"纯美之极,且兼得朦胧之美感"。这首精巧别致的回文诗《慢慢地》果然透着淡淡的朦胧之美。

2. A Christmas Tree[①]

William Burford

Star

If you are

A love compassionate,

You will walk with us this year.

We face a glacial distance[②], who are here

Huddld[③]

At your feet.

【诗人简介】威廉·斯凯里·伯福德(William skellg Burford,1927—2004),当代美国诗人。著有《一个开始:诗歌集》(*A Beginning Poems*)、《现在的人》(*Man Now*)和一个世界(*A World*)等。

【注释】

① 此诗由美国得克萨斯诗人威廉·伯福德(William Burford,1927—2004)所作。

② a glacial distance:冰河时代的距离。

③ huddld:正确的拼法应该是 huddled,意即"蜷缩着的"。在这里,诗人故意略去了字母 e,以突出"拥挤不堪"的效果。

【作品赏析】

形体诗(即英文所谓的 Shape Poetry or Concrete Poetry or Visual Poetry)是诗歌中的一种特殊类型。诗人在创作形体诗的时候,通常会把文字和绘画艺术的某些元素融合起来,将诗歌映射成图像,使读者在欣赏诗歌的时候不仅能够得到视觉的享受,更能通过这种形体使意义升华,从而达到内在美和外在美的统一。西方形体诗的源头最早可以追溯到古希腊。大约在公元 4 世纪以前,一些古希腊的田园诗人就已经尝试把诗行排成斧头或鸡蛋等形状。在英国文学史上,这种诗体最早出现在 16 世纪,后来曾一度广为流行。赫伯特(George Herbert)、赫利克(Robert Herrick)、伯吞汉姆(George Puttenham)和夸尔斯(Francis Quarles)等都曾写过不少形体诗。其中,尤以赫伯特的《祭坛》(*The Altar*)和《复活节的翅膀》(*Easter Wings*)最为有名。

形体诗绝不是"形体+诗"的简单叠加,而是"形体"与"诗"的完美结合,是形式与内容的有机统一,是有形与无形的水乳交融。

第八章
另类的诗歌

作为视觉诗的一个分支,形体诗常常给诗歌罩上一层朦胧的色彩。正所谓"诗中有画,画中有诗",形体诗的独特构思赋予了诗歌灵动之美,也给读者留下了无限遐想的空间。当然,形体诗也存在一些天然的缺陷。比如,它们往往不适合优美地朗诵,缺乏韵律之美,等等。

《圣诞树》是威廉·伯福德所作的一首著名的形体诗。正如诗歌的题目所表明的,该诗从外观上来看酷似一棵圣诞树。第一行的 star 给人的感觉应该是树的顶端,也就是树梢。第五行是该诗最长的一行,就像是枝叶繁茂的树身。最后的两行,可以看出是树的底部。中间的二、三和四行也是按照长度由短到长排列,和树干以及树的底部的构建相似。从诗的结构来看,俨然是一棵圣诞树的形状。显而易见,这首诗所要表达的内容是关于圣诞日的。在西方,每当圣诞来临之际,人们会向全能的耶稣祈祷,希望来年能够带来好运。这首形体诗恰好形象地描绘了人们向上帝祈祷的情景。诗人把 star 放在最上方,既符合一般圣诞树的装饰习惯,同时又是一种隐喻手法。他把 star 比喻成充满"仁爱"和"关怀"的上帝,苦难深重的人们则蜷缩在他的脚下,对着他膜拜和祈祷。为了使诗歌的形式与意义浑然一体,作者对每一个单词的使用都进行了反复的斟酌和推敲,最好的体现便是在对 Huddld 一词的处理上。这个词初看会误以为是拼写错误,但是经过细致的揣摩和体会,读者应能觉察到诗人的用意所在。诗人省去了字母 e,达到了特殊的效果。Huddld 这个特殊的单词中竟然有多达五个带长柄的字母,它们就像五个瘦弱的人蜷缩在一棵圣诞树下虔诚地进行祈祷,构成了一副狭小、拥挤的画面,点出了底层百姓苦不堪言的生存状态。他们在发出无声的呐喊,在祈求上帝赐予恩泽。

总之,在这首诗歌中,诗人通过字、词和句的特殊排列组合,营造出了强烈的视觉冲击效果,大大增强了作品的表现力。

3. Jazz Fantasia[①]
Carl Sandburg

Drum on your drums, batter on your banjoes[②],
    sob on the long cool winding saxophones.
        Go to it, O jazzmen.

Sling your knuckles on the bottoms of the happy
    tin pans, let your trombones[③] ooze[④], and go husha-
        husha-hush with the slippery sand-paper.

Moan like an autumn wind high in the lonesome treetops,
    moan soft like you wanted somebody terrible, cry like a
racing car slipping away from a motorcycle cop, bang-bang!
you jazzmen, bang altogether drums, traps[⑤], banjoes, horns,
    tin cans — make two people fight on the top of a stairway
    and scratch each other's eyes in a clinch[⑥] tumbling down
        the stairs.

Can the rough stuff ... now a Mississippi steamboat pushes
    up the night river with a hoo-hoo-hoo-oo ... and the green
    lanterns calling to the high soft stars ... a red moon rides

on the humps of the low river hills … go to it, O jazzmen.

【注释】

① 此诗选自美国诗人卡尔·桑德堡(Carl Sandburg,1878—1967)于1920年出版的诗集《烟与钢》(*Smoke and Steel*)。

② banjo：美国民间流行的班卓琴,类似吉他,有四根或五根弦。

③ trombone：长号。

④ ooze：原指液体慢慢渗出,此处指音乐缓缓升起、绵延不绝。

⑤ trap：爵士音乐中使用的打击乐器。

⑥ clinch：原指相互扭打搂抱在一起,这里是一种模仿音乐效果的用法。

【作品赏析】

"情动于中而形于言,言之不足,故嗟叹之,嗟叹之不足,故咏歌之,咏歌之不足,不知手之舞之,足之蹈之也",《毛诗大序》中的这句话证明了诗与歌之间的同源关系。所谓诗歌,既是诗,又是歌,更是诗和歌的有机结合。中国古典诗词如此,在西方文学传统中,诗与乐之间的紧密联系也由来已久。西方文化起源于古希腊,古希腊神话中的宙斯作为众神之神,他手下的抒情诗女神手里就抱着一把琴,可见,诗与歌在西方人心目中原本难分彼此。到了近代和现代,虽然诗歌的发展经历了无数的变革,但诗与歌之间的联系仍一如既往地紧密,甚至更为紧密。特别是随着诗歌越来越走向大众,各种诗歌朗诵会、赛诗会、诗歌品赏和推介活动等把诗与歌的结合推向了高点。

爵士乐是一种源自美国黑人的民间音乐,其特点为节奏强烈、调子激越昂扬。20世纪20年代，美国诗人林赛（Vachel Lindsay）、庞德（Ezra Pound）、卡明斯（E.E. Cummings）、克莱（Hart Crane）以及后来的休斯（Langston Hughes）等人率先尝试在诗歌中揉入爵士乐的元素，创作出了最初的"爵士诗"。桑德堡也是"爵士诗"创作的先锋成员之一，他对爵士乐的兴趣很大程度上是基于他对民间音乐和民俗文化的喜爱，这首《爵士幻想曲》即是他的代表性作品。

在这首诗歌中，令人印象最为深刻的是贯穿全篇的音乐符号。作品中先后出现的各类乐器就有 drum, banjo, saxophone, trap, horn 和 trombone 等，甚至连 tin pan, tin can 和 slippery sandpaper 等也被用来当作发声的乐器。此外，与这些乐器相配套的表示动作的词汇 drum, batter, sob, sling, ooze, moan, cry, bang, fight 和 scratch 等给人的感觉则是飘忽灵动、充满想象力。不同的乐器、不同的演奏动作，永远不变的是萦绕耳际的"爵士幻想曲"。它们或高亢嘹亮，或低回深沉，或狂野不羁，或忧伤哀怨同，为了进一步渲染气氛、烘托效果，诗人还多次使用了"husha-husha-hush，bang-bang，hoo-hoo-hoo-oo"等拟声词，简直把爵士乐的氛围调制到无以复加的地步，为读者奉上了一道不折不扣的音乐盛宴。如果说爱伦·坡曾因其诗歌中的音乐性而被称为 Jingleman 的话，那么，桑德堡似乎应该被称为 Jazzman，他的诗歌里面的音乐更狂野、更有个性。

桑德堡出身于劳动阶层，并以普通劳动者的代言人自居，他的诗有着浓厚的美国民族特质和泥土气息。这首《爵士幻想曲》不但充满了狂野的音乐元素，同时感情的表达也十分细腻，它是忙碌的城市生活的真实写照，反映了生活在城市里的人们的生存状态。

4. Two Stones with One Bird[①]

Charles Bernstein

Re-
demption

comes

&

redemp-
tion

goes

but

trans-
ience

is

here

for-
ever.

【诗人简介】查尔斯·伯恩斯坦(Charles Bernstein, 1950—   ),美国艺术与科学院院士、美国语言诗派的重要诗人及诗歌理论家,著有30部诗集。

【注释】

① 此诗最初刊载在2008年6月的《诗歌》(Poetry)杂志。

【作品赏析】

语言诗自20世纪70年代开始在美国诗坛崛起,以同时期创刊的两本刊物 *This* 和 *L＝A＝N＝G＝U＝A＝G＝E* 为标志。语言诗人反叛正统的诗歌形式,采用一切可能的手段打破语言和诗歌的规约,打破逻辑意义,消解连贯的声音,切断语言与现实的联系,把语言对所指的关注引向语言本身。语言诗的代表人物主要有查尔斯·伯恩斯坦、布鲁斯·安德鲁斯、詹姆斯·谢里和罗恩·西利曼等,其中现任教于宾夕法尼亚大学的查尔斯·伯恩斯坦教授是该诗派的领军人物。他不但创作了许多语言诗,而且还为语言诗的发展提供了理论依据。他的作品机智幽默,看似漫不经心却处处充满深意。迄今为止,伯恩斯坦的诗作已在500多家刊物发表,还被翻译成多国文字。

《二石一鸟》(*Two Stones with One Bird*)是伯恩斯坦教授在2008年发表的一首小诗。单看此诗的标题,就足以令读者细细玩味一番。"一石二鸟"作为耳熟能详的成语,无论在中国还是英美文化的语境中早已被大家接受。所谓"一石二鸟",或者是"一箭双雕"、"一举两得",指的大概是一种讨巧的行为,也就是说以尽量少的付出和代价而谋求获得双倍的收益。但是,在这里作者却反其道而行之,把自己的诗歌命名为"二石一鸟"。显然,作者有自己的考虑。那么,这"二石"到底是指什么,那个"一鸟"又代表了什么呢?通读全诗,不难发现 Redemption comes 和 redemption goes 似乎就是那"二石",而紧接着的 transience 自然代表"一鸟"。尽管这首小诗的文字编排有些奇特,标题颇有点故弄玄虚的味道,但是,要真正抓住"二石"和"一鸟"似乎并不太难。至于透过那"二石"和"一鸟",诗人究竟想告诉读者什么,这就是仁者见仁、智者见智了。语言诗作为后现代主义文学的一个品种曾经颇受争议,但

第八章
另类的诗歌

是，有一点是十分明确的，那就是语言诗人重视读者的参与，强调由读者来阐释作品的意义。也许，诗人的用意在于提醒人们生命的短暂和宝贵。也许，他不过是在哀叹忏悔和救赎的徒劳，并告诫人们应该学会真实地生活。也许，当你读过无数遍之后，在某一天的傍晚再次想起这首不起眼的小诗的时候，你又会有新的发现。这就是诗歌的魅力，语言诗也不例外。

小 结

所谓"另类的诗歌"是一个有趣的话题。实际上，但凡诗歌，不管其形式、内容或具体的表现手段如何千差万别，只要能吸引读者的目光、能打动读者的心灵、能经受住时间的考验，那么，它就应该是好诗。

玛丽·柯勒律治的《慢慢地》是一首回文诗，它在形式上的独具一格已无须赘言。作为一名活跃在19世纪晚期的女性诗人，她勇于把实验性的元素揉入自己的创作之中，实属难能可贵。更加值得肯定的是，《慢慢地》并非一首单纯卖弄技巧的花哨的作品，它还包含着丰富的真情实感，正是这首诗歌的回文特征强化了作品所要表达的恋人之间依依惜别的主题。威廉·伯福德的《圣诞树》被认为是一首典型的"形体诗"。它的圣诞树造型亲切、生动，令人印象深刻。但是，通读全篇，读者却轻松不起来。相反，他们会感到一阵阵的寒意从背后袭来，会感到沉重和无所适从。同样是不起眼的小诗，如果说柯勒律治以情感的细腻绵密而动人，那么，伯福德则胜在深刻凝重。查尔斯·伯恩斯坦的《二石一鸟》也是一首有趣的作品，它的形式已足够特立独行，而在容量上则更加"迷你"，仅有10个经过精心排列的单词和一个连接符号。不过，伯恩斯坦可不是为了追求形式而形式，他的这首小诗在主题的深度和广度上可以说不输任何一部大部头的作品。而要真正把握它非凡的意义,恐怕还需要读者沉入其中,反复咀嚼和体会,这也是语言诗对读者提出的挑战之一。从某种意义上来说,伯恩斯坦的这首诗是以奇制胜、以少胜多的范本。至于桑德堡,一般而言,他的诗风以雄壮和大气磅礴而得名,同时也经常给人以亲切、自然的印象。这里所选的《爵士幻想曲》是一个比较特殊的例子,代表了桑德堡诗歌创作的另一个侧面。不过,作品中透过各种音响效果所反映的城市生活的场景倒是符合诗人一贯的追求。正如许多评论家所指出的,桑德堡是属于大众的诗人。

本章是我们这本"英美诗歌导读"的最后一个部分,所选的四首诗歌被冠以"另类的诗歌"的称谓。这些作品,因其在某一方面或几个方面所展现出的独特性,显得与传统意义上的诗歌有所不同,故而被归入此列。不过,需要加以说明的是,这里的"另类"一词并非贬义,它只是一种临时的指称,甚或还可能是不太恰当的指称。事实上,在英美诗歌的发展过程中,大胆的叛逆、反传统和刻意的另类创新比比皆是,有些甚至到了极端和荒诞的地步,但这些并非本书考察的范围。我们的目的是希望借助这些作品使读者对诗歌的弹性功能和无限可能有一个基本的认识,以便帮助读者恰如其分地把握英美诗歌的总体风貌。

扩展阅读篇目

The New Poetry Handbook by Mark Strand
Bells of Gray Crystal by Edith Sitwell
To the Virgins, to Make Much of Time by Robert Herrick
To His Coy Mistress by Andrew Marvell
Carpe Diem by Robert Frost

第八章
另类的诗歌

On the Way to Language by Michael Palmer
We Real Cool by Gwendolyn Brooks
The Weary Blues by Langston Hughes
I Carry Your Heart with Me by E. E. Cummings
Slam Time by Raymong Ngomane

附 录

诗 人 谈 诗

The forms of things unknown, the poet's pen
Turns them to shapes, and gives to airy nothing
A local habitation and a name.
William Shakespeare (1564—1616)

Poetry is the music of the soul, and, above all, of great and feeling souls.
Voltaire (1694—1778)

The ending of writing is to instruct; the end of poetry is to instruct by pleasing.
Samuel Johnson (1709—1784)

Poetry is thoughts that breathe, and words that burn.
Thomas Gray (1716—1771)

A man should hear a little music, read a little poetry, and see a fine picture every day of his life, in order that worldly cares may not obliterate the sense of the beautiful which God has

implanted in the human soul.
Johann Wolfgang von Goethe (1749—1832)

I have said that poetry is the spontaneous overflow of powerful feelings: it takes its origin from emotion recollected in tranquility: the emotion is contemplated till, by a species of reaction, the tranquility gradually disappears, and an emotion, kindred to that which was before the subject of contemplation, is gradually produced, and does itself actually exist in the mind.
William Wordsworth (1770—1850)

I wish our clever young poets would remember my homely definitions of prose and poetry; that is prose; words in their best order;— poetry; the best words in the best order.
S. T. Coleridge (1772—1834)

The Genius of Poetry must work out its own salvation in a man; it cannot be matured by law and percept, but by sensation and watchfulness in itself.
John Keats (1795—1821)

Yet poetry, though the last and finest result, is a natural fruit. As naturally as the oak bears an acorn, and the vine a gourd, man bears a poem, either spoken or done. It is the chief and most memorable success, for history is but a prose narrative of poetic deeds.

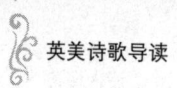

Henry David Thoreau (1817—1862)

To have great poets there must be great audiences too.

Walt Whitman (1819—1892)

Poetry is at bottom a criticism of life; that the greatness of a poet lies in his powerful and beautiful application of ideas to life—to the question: How to live.

Matthew Arnold (1822—1888)

If I read a book and it makes my whole body so cold no fire ever can warm me I know that is poetry. If I feel physically as if the top of my head were taken off, I know that is poetry. These are the only way I know it. Is there any other way?

Emily Dickinson (1830—1886)

It is the job of poetry to clean up our word-clogged reality by creating silences around things.

Stephen Mallarme (1842—1898)

There are three things, after all, that a poem must reach: the eye, the ear, and what we may call the heart or the mind. It is most important of all to reach the heart of the reader.

Robert Frost (1874—1963)

Poetry is a projection across silence of cadences arranged to break that silence with definite intentions of echoes, syllables, wave lengths.

Carl Sandburg (1878—1967)

The poet is the priest of the invisible.

Wallace Stevens (1879—1955)

Use no superfluous word, no adjective, which does not reveal something. Don't use such an expression as "dim land of peace". It dulls the image. It mixes an abstraction with the concrete. It comes from the writer's not realising that the natural object is always the *adequate* symbol. Go in fear of abstractions.

Ezra Pound (1885—1972)

Poetry is the art of creating imaginary gardens with real toads.

Marianne Moore (1887—1972)

A poem should not mean.
But be.

Archibald MacLeish (1892—1982)

If there's no money in poetry, neither is there poetry in money.

Robert Graves (1895—1985)

I grew up in this town, my poetry was born between the hill and the river, it took its voice from the rain, and like the timber, it steeped itself in the forests.

Pablo Neruda (1904—1973)

The poem ... is a little myth of man's capacity of making life meaningful. And in the end, the poem is not a thing we see— it is, rather, a light by which we may see—and what we see is life.

Robert Penn Warren (1905—1989)

Poetry is, above all, an approach to the truth of feeling ... A fine poem will seize your imagination intellectually—that is, when you reach it, you will reach it intellectually too—but the way is through emotion, through what we call feeling.

Muriel Rukeyser (1913—1980)

Poetry is what in a poem makes you laugh, cry, prickle, be silent, makes your toe nails twinkle, makes you want to do this or that or nothing, makes you know that you are alone in the unknown world, that your bliss and suffering is forever shared and forever all your own.

Dylan Thomas (1914—1953)

Poetry is like making a joke. If you get one word wrong at the end of a joke, you've lost the whole thing.

W. S. Merwin (1927—   )

If you know what you are going to write when you're writing a poem, it's going to be average.

        Derek Walcott (1930—)

For women ... poetry is not a luxury. It is a vital necessity of our existence. It forms the quality of light within which we can predicate our hopes and dreams toward survival and change, first made into language, then into idea, then into more tangible action. Poetry is the way we help give name to the nameless so it can be thought. The farthest horizons of our hopes and fears are cobbled by our poems, carved from the rock experiences of our daily lives.

        Audre Lorde (1934—1992)

Poetry is an ancient art or technology: older than the computer, older than print, older than writing and indeed, though some may find this surprising, much older than prose. I presume that the technology of poetry, using the human body as its medium, evolved for specific uses; to hold things in memory, both within and beyond the individual life span; to achieve intensity and sensuous appeal; to express feelings and ideas rapidly and memorably; to share those feelings and ideas with companions, and also with the dead and with those to come after us.

        Robert Pinsky (1940—)

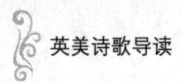

Poetry is language at its most distilled and most powerful.

Rita Dove (1952—)

Section I: Part IV

Poetry in general seems to have sprung from two causes, each of them lying deep in our nature. First, the instinct of imitation is implanted in man from childhood, one difference between him and other animals being that he is the most imitative of living creatures, and through imitation learns his earliest lessons; and no less universal is the pleasure felt in things imitated. We have evidence of this in the facts of experience. Objects which in themselves we view with pain, we delight to contemplate when reproduced with minute fidelity: such as the forms of the most ignoble animals and of dead bodies. The cause of this again is, that to learn gives the liveliest pleasure, not only to philosophers but to men in general; whose capacity, however, of learning is more limited. Thus the reason why men enjoy seeing a likeness is, that in contemplating it they find themselves learning or inferring, and saying perhaps, "Ah, that is he." For if you happen not to have seen the original, the pleasure will be due not to the imitation as such, but to the execution, the coloring, or some such other cause.

Imitation, then, is one instinct of our nature. Next, there is the instinct for "harmony" and rhythm, meters being manifestly sections of rhythm. Persons, therefore, starting with this natural gift developed by degrees their special aptitudes, till their rude improvisations gave birth to Poetry ...

Part IX

It is, moreover, evident from what has been said, that it is not the function of the poet to relate what has happened, but what may happen—what is possible according to the law of probability or necessity. The poet and the historian differ not by writing in verse or in prose. The work of Herodotus might be put into verse, and it would still be a species of history, with meter no less than without it. The true difference is that one relates what has happened, the other what may happen. Poetry, therefore, is a more philosophical and a higher thing than history: for poetry tends to express the universal, history the particular. By the universal I mean how a person of a certain type on occasion speak or act, according to the law of probability or necessity; and it is this universality at which poetry aims in the names she attaches to the personages.

From *Poetics* by **Aristotle (384 BC—322 BC)**

Translated by S. H. Butcher

Poetry is indeed something divine. It is at once the centre and circumference of knowledge; it is that which comprehends all science, and that to which all science must be referred. It is at the same time the root and blossom of all other systems of thought; it is that from which all spring, and that which adorns all; and that which, if blighted, denies the fruit and the seed, and withholds from the barren world the nourishment and the succession of the scions of the tree of life. It is the perfect and consummate surface and bloom of all things; it is as the odor and the color of the rose to the texture of the elements which compose it, as the form and splendor of unfaded beauty to the secrets of anatomy and corruption. What were virtue, love, patriotism, friendship—what were the scenery of this beautiful universe which we inhabit; what were our consolations on this side of the grave—and what were our aspirations beyond it, if poetry did not ascend to bring light and fire from those eternal regions where the owl-winged faculty of calculation dare not ever soar? Poetry is not like reasoning, a power to be exerted according to the determination of the will. A man cannot say, "I will compose poetry." The greatest poet even cannot say it; for the mind in creation is as a fading coal, which some invisible influence, like an inconstant wind, awakens to transitory brightness; this power arises from within, like the color of a flower which fades and changes as it is developed, and the conscious portions of our natures are unprophetic either of its approach or its departure. Could this influence be durable in its original purity and force, it is impossible to predict the greatness of the results; but when composition begins, inspiration is already on the decline, and the most glorious poetry that has ever been communicated to the world is probably a feeble shadow of the original conceptions of the poet.

...

Poetry is the record of the best and happiest moments of the happiest and best minds. We are aware of evanescent visitations of thought and feeling sometimes associated with place or person, sometimes regarding our own mind alone, and always arising unforeseen and departing unbidden, but elevating and delightful beyond all expression: so that even in the desire and the regret they leave, there cannot but be pleasure, participating as it does in the nature of its object. It is as it were the interpretation of a diviner nature through our own; but its footsteps are like those of a wind over the sea, which the coming calm erases, and whose traces remain only as on the wrinkled sand which paves it. These and corresponding conditions of being are experienced principally by those of the most delicate sensibility and the most enlarged imagination; and the state of mind produced by them is at war with every base desire. The enthusiasm of virtue, love, patriotism, and friendship is essentially linked with such emotions; and whilst they last, self appears as what it is, an atom to a universe. Poets are not only subject to these experiences as spirits of the most refined organization, but they can color all that they combine with the evanescent hues of this ethereal world; a word, a trait in the representation of a scene or a passion will touch the enchanted chord, and reanimate, in those who have ever experienced these emotions, the sleeping, the cold, the buried image of the past. Poetry thus makes immortal all that is best and most beautiful in the world; it arrests the vanishing apparitions which haunt the interlunations of life, and veiling them, or in language or in form, sends them forth among mankind, bearing sweet news of kindred joy to those with whom their sisters abide—abide, because there is no portal of expression from the caverns of the spirit which they inhabit into the universe of things. Poetry redeems from decay the visitations of the divinity in man.

Poetry turns all things to loveliness; it exalts the beauty of that which is most beautiful, and it adds beauty to that which is most deformed; it marries exultation and horror, grief and pleasure, eternity and change; it subdues to union under its light yoke all irreconcilable things. It transmutes all that it touches, and every form moving within the radiance of its presence is changed by wondrous sympathy to an incarnation of the spirit which it breathes; its secret alchemy turns to potable gold the poisonous waters which flow from death through life; it strips the veil of familiarity from the world, and lays bare the naked and sleeping beauty, which is the spirit of its forms...

A poet, as he is the author to others of the highest wisdom, pleasure, virtue, and glory, so he ought personally to be the happiest, the best, the wisest, and the most illustrious of men. As to his glory, let time be challenged to declare whether the fame of any other institutor of human life be comparable to that of a poet. That he is the wisest, the happiest, and the best, inasmuch as he is a poet, is equally incontrovertible: the greatest poets have been men of the most spotless virtue, of the most consummate prudence, and, if we would look into the interior of their lives, the most fortunate of men: and the exceptions, as they regard those who possessed the poetic faculty in a high yet inferior degree, will be found on consideration to confine rather than destroy the rule.

...

Poets are the hierophants of an unapprehended inspiration; the mirrors of the gigantic shadows which futurity casts upon the present; the words which express what they understand not; the trumpets which sing to battle, and feel not what they inspire; the influence which is moved not, but moves. Poets are the unacknowledged legislators of the world.

From *A Defence of Poetry* by **Percy Bysshe Shelley** (1792—1822)

Dividing the world of mind into its three most immediately obvious distinctions, we have the Pure Intellect, Taste, and the Moral Sense. I place Taste in the middle, because it is just this position which in the mind it occupies. It holds intimate relations with either extreme; but from the Moral Sense is separated by so faint a difference that Aristotle has not hesitated to place some of its operations among the virtues themselves. Nevertheless we find the offices of the trio marked with a sufficient distinction. Just as the Intellect concerns itself with Truth, so Taste informs us of the Beautiful, while the

Moral Sense is regardful of Duty. Of this latter, while Conscience teaches the obligation, and Reason the expediency, Taste contents herself with displaying the charms:—waging war upon Vice solely on the ground of her deformity—her disproportion—her animosity to the fitting, to the appropriate, to the harmonious—in a word, to Beauty.

An immortal instinct deep within the spirit of man is thus plainly a sense of the Beautiful. This it is which administers to his delight in the manifold forms, and sounds, and odors and sentiments amid which he exists. And just as the lily is repeated in the lake, or the eyes of Amaryllis in the mirror, so is the mere oral or written repetition of these forms, and sounds, and colors, and odors, and sentiments a duplicate source of delight. But this mere repetition is not poetry. He who shall simply sing, with however glowing enthusiasm, or with however vivid a truth of description, of the sights, and sounds, and odors, and colors, and sentiments which greet him in common with all mankind—he, I say, has yet faded to prove his divine title. There is still a something in the distance which he has been unable to attain. We have still a thirst unquenchable, to allay which he has not shown us the crystal springs. This thirst belongs to the immortality of Man. It is at once a consequence and an indication of his perennial existence. It is the desire of the moth for the star. It is no mere appreciation of the Beauty before us, but a wild effort to reach the Beauty above. Inspired by an ecstatic prescience of the glories beyond the grave, we struggle by multiform combinations among the things and thoughts of Time to attain a portion of that Loveliness whose very elements perhaps appertain to eternity alone. And thus when by Poetry, or when by Music, the most entrancing of the poetic moods, we find ourselves melted into tears, we weep then, not as the Abbate Gravina supposes, through excess of pleasure, but through a certain petulant, impatient sorrow at our inability to grasp now, wholly, here on earth, at once and for ever, those divine and rapturous joys of which through the poem, or through the music, we attain to but brief and indeterminate glimpses.

The struggle to apprehend the supernal Loveliness—this struggle, on the part of souls fittingly constituted—has given to the world all that which it (the world) has ever been enabled at once to understand and to feel as poetic ...

Thus, although in a very cursory and imperfect manner, I have endeavoured to convey to you my conception of the Poetic Principle. It has been my purpose to suggest that, while this principle itself is strictly and simply the Human Aspiration for Supernal Beauty, the manifestation of the Principle is always found in an elevating excitement of the soul, quite independent of that passion which is the intoxication of the Heart, or of that truth which is the satisfaction of the Reason. For in regard to passion, alas! its tendency is to degrade rather than to elevate the Soul. Love, on the contrary-Love-the true, the divine Eros— the Uranian as distinguished from the Dionnan Venus —

is unquestionably the purest and truest of all poetical themes. And in regard to Truth, if, to be sure, through the attainment of a truth we are led to perceive a harmony where none was apparent before, we experience at once the true poetical effect; but this effect is referable to the harmony alone, and not in the least degree to the truth which merely served to render the harmony manifest.

From *The Poetic Principle* by **Edgar Allan Poe** (1809—1849)

Part I
IN English writing we seldom speak of tradition, though we occasionally apply its name in deploring its absence. We cannot refer to "the tradition" or to "a tradition"; at most, we employ the adjective in saying that the poetry of So-and-so is "traditional" or even "too traditional". Seldom, perhaps, does the word appear except in a phrase of censure. If otherwise, it is vaguely approbative, with the implication, as to the work approved, of some pleasing archeological reconstruction. You can hardly make the word agreeable to English ears without this comfortable reference to the reassuring science of archeology.
Certainly the word is not likely to appear in our appreciations of living or dead writers. Every nation, every race, has not only its own creative, but its own critical turn of mind; and is even more oblivious of the shortcomings and limitations of its critical habits than of those of its creative genius. We know, or think we know, from the enormous mass of critical writing that has

appeared in the French language the critical method or habit of the French; we only conclude (we are such unconscious people) that the French are "more critical" than we, and sometimes even plume ourselves a little with the fact, as if the French were the less spontaneous. Perhaps they are; but we might remind ourselves that criticism is as inevitable as breathing, and that we should be none the worse for articulating what passes in our minds when we read a book and feel an emotion about it, for criticizing our own minds in their work of criticism. One of the facts that might come to light in this process is our tendency to insist, when we praise a poet, upon those aspects of his work in which he least resembles anyone else. In these aspects or parts of his work we pretend to find what is individual, what is the peculiar essence of the man. We dwell with satisfaction upon the poet's difference from his predecessors, especially his immediate predecessors; we endeavour to find something that can be isolated in order to be enjoyed.

Whereas if we approach a poet without this prejudice we shall often find that not only the best, but the most individual parts of his work may be those in which the dead poets, his ancestors, assert their immortality most vigorously. And I do not mean the impressionable period of adolescence, but the period of full maturity.

Yet if the only form of tradition, of handing down, consisted in following the ways of the immediate generation before us in a blind or timid adherence to its successes, "tradition" should positively be discouraged. We have seen many such simple currents soon lost in the sand; and novelty is better than repetition. Tradition is a matter of much wider significance. It cannot be inherited, and if you want it you must obtain it by great labour. It involves, in the first place, the historical sense, which we may call nearly indispensable to anyone who would continue to be a poet beyond his twenty-fifth year; and the historical sense involves a perception, not only of the pastness of the past, but of its presence; the historical sense compels a man to write not merely with his own generation in his bones, but with a feeling that the whole of the literature of Europe from Homer and within it the whole of the literature of his own country has a simultaneous existence and composes a simultaneous order. This historical sense, which is a sense of the timeless as well as of the temporal and of the timeless and of the temporal together, is what makes a writer traditional. And it is at the same time what makes a writer most acutely conscious of his place in time, of his contemporaneity.

No poet, no artist of any art, has his complete meaning alone. His significance, his appreciation is the appreciation of his relation to the dead poets and artists. You cannot value him alone; you must set him, for contrast and comparison, among the dead. I mean this as a principle of aesthetic, not merely historical, criticism. The necessity that he shall conform, that he shall cohere, is not one-sided; what happens when a new work of art is created is something that happens simultaneously to all the works of art which preceded it. The existing monuments form an ideal order among themselves, which is modified by the introduction of the new (the really new) work of art among them. The existing order is complete before the new work arrives; for order to persist after the supervention of novelty, the whole existing order must be, if ever so slightly, altered; and so the relations, proportions, values of each work of art toward the whole are readjusted; and this is conformity between the old and the new. Whoever has approved this idea of order, of the form of European, of English literature, will not find it preposterous that the past should be altered by the present as much as the present is directed by the past. And the poet who is aware of this will be aware of great difficulties and responsibilities.

In a peculiar sense he will be aware also that he must inevitably be judged by the standards of the past. I say judged, not amputated, by them; not judged to be as good as, or worse or better than, the dead; and certainly not judged by the canons of dead critics. It is a judgment, a comparison, in which two things are measured by each other. To conform merely would be for the new work not really to conform at all; it would not be new, and would therefore not be a work of art. And we do not quite say that the new is more valuable because it fits in; but its fitting in is a test of its value—a test, it is true, which can only be slowly and cautiously applied, for we are none of us infallible judges of conformity. We say: it appears to conform, and is perhaps individual, or it appears individual, and may conform; but we are hardly likely to find that it is one and not the other.

To proceed to a more intelligible exposition of the relation of the poet to the past: he can neither take the past as a lump, an indiscriminate bolus, nor can he form himself wholly on one or two private admirations, nor can he form himself wholly upon one preferred period. The first course is inadmissible, the second is an important experience of youth, and the third is a pleasant and highly desirable supplement. The poet must be very conscious of the main current, which does not at all flow invariably through the most distinguished reputations. He must be quite aware of the obvious fact that art never improves, but that the material of art is never quite the same. He must be aware that the mind of Europe—The mind of his own country—a mind which he learns in time to be much more important than his own private mind—is a mind which changes, and that this change is a development which abandons nothing en route, which does not superannuate either Shakespeare, or Homer, or the rock drawing of the Magdalenian draughtsmen. That this development, refinement perhaps, complication certainly, is not, from the point of view of the artist, any improvement. Perhaps not even an improvement from the point of view of the psychologist or not to the extent which we imagine; perhaps only in the end based upon a complication in economics and machinery. But the difference between the present and the past is that the conscious present is an awareness of the past in a way and to an extent which the past's awareness of itself cannot show.

Someone said:"The dead writers are remote from us because we know so much more than they did." Precisely, and they are that which we know.

I am alive to a usual objection to what is clearly part of my programme for the metier of poetry. The objection is that the doctrine requires a ridiculous amount of erudition (pedantry), a claim which can be rejected by appeal to the lives of poets in any pantheon. It will even be affirmed that much learning deadens or perverts poetic sensibility. While, however, we persist in believing that a poet ought to know as much as will not encroach upon his necessary receptivity and necessary laziness, it is not desirable to confine knowledge to whatever can be put into a useful shape for examinations, drawing-rooms, or the still more pretentious modes of publicity. Some can absorb knowledge, the more tardy must sweat for it. Shakespeare acquired more essential history from Plutarch than most men could from the whole British Museum. What is to be insisted upon is that the poet must develop or procure the onsciousness of the past and that he should continue to develop this consciousness throughout his career.

What happens is a continual surrender of himself as he is at the moment to something which is more valuable. The progress of an artist is a continual self-sacrifice, a continual extinction of personality.

There remains to define this process of depersonalization and its relation to the sense of tradition. It is in this depersonalization that art may be said to approach the condition of science. I shall, therefore, invite you to consider, as a suggestive analogy, the action which takes place when a bit of finely filiated platinum is introduced into a chamber containing oxygen and sulphur dioxide.

From *Tradition and the Individual Talent*

By T. S. Eliot (1888—1965)